PADDINGTON
AT LARGE

PADDINGTON
AT LARGE

by MICHAEL BOND

illustrated by PEGGY FORTNUM

Brought to you by
The Daily Telegraph

First published in Great Britain
by William Collins Sons and Co. Ltd. in 1962
This edition first published by Collins in 1998

Collins is an imprint of
HarperCollinsPublishers Ltd, 77–85 Fulham Palace Road,
Hammersmith, London W6 8JB

The HarperCollins website address is
www.**fire**and**water**.com

ISBN 978-0-00-779231-3

Printed in Great Britain by
Clays Ltd, St Ives plc

CONTENTS

Chapter One

PADDINGTON BREAKS THE PEACE

"I know I keep on saying it," exclaimed Mrs Brown, as she placed an extremely large vegetable marrow on the kitchen scales, "but I'm sure Paddington must have been born with green paws. Have you seen this one? He's beaten his best by over half a pound."

"Hmm," said Mrs Bird. "Well, I'll grant you one thing, green paws are better than idle ones and at least gardening keeps him busy. We haven't had an upset for weeks now."

The Browns' housekeeper hastily touched wood as her eyes followed the progress of a small brown figure clad in a shapeless hat and an equally disreputable-looking duffle coat as it made its way down the garden path before disappearing into a potting shed behind the raspberry canes.

Mrs Bird was never very happy about any of Paddington's activities which took him out of her sight for too long a time, and Paddington's interest in gardening had lasted much too long for her peace of mind.

All the same, even Mrs Bird had to admit that for some time past things had been remarkably peaceful at number thirty-two Windsor Gardens.

It had all started when Paddington arrived home from the market one day carrying a giant packet of assorted seeds which he'd bought for the bargain price of five pence. At the time it had seemed such good value for money that Mr Brown had been only too pleased to let him have a corner of the garden, and for several evenings afterwards Paddington had been kept very busy counting the seeds, making sure none of them were stuck to his paws as he sorted them into separate piles in order of size before he planted them.

Only Mrs Bird had been full of forebodings. "Woe betide the man in the shop if they don't all come up," she remarked when she noticed the seed packet had been marked down from fifteen pence. "I can see there'll be some nasty scenes."

But despite Mrs Bird's misgivings, within a week or two the first of the seeds began to sprout and in no time at all 'Paddington's Patch' was such a blaze of colour it soon put the rest of the garden to shame.

From that moment on Paddington spent most of his spare time out of doors, and when he began supplying the household with vegetables as well as flowers everyone had to agree with Mrs Brown that he must have been born with green paws.

"I must say the garden is a picture at the moment," she continued, as she turned to help Mrs Bird with the washing-up. "Even Mr Curry called out this morning and said how nice it looks."

"If I know Mr Curry," said Mrs Bird darkly, "he was probably after something. He doesn't say things like that without a very good reason."

"Perhaps he wants some cheap vegetables," said Mrs Brown. "You know how mean he is."

"He'll be lucky with that bear," replied Mrs Bird. "And quite right too, seeing the state his own garden's in. It's a disgrace."

Mr Curry's lawn was very overgrown with weeds and Mrs Bird held strong views about the way the seeds blew over the fence whenever there was a strong wind.

"Funnily enough," said Mrs Brown, "I think he was just getting his lawnmower out when he spoke to me. Perhaps he's going to make a start."

"Not before time," snorted Mrs Bird. "And I shall believe it when I see it. He's much more likely to give the job to some poor bob-a-job-week scout than do it himself."

Mrs Bird gave the washing-up several nasty jabs with her mop, but if she had been able to see Mr Curry as she spoke she would probably have snorted even louder, for at that moment the Browns' neighbour was peering over the fence at Paddington with a very cunning expression on his face.

Unaware of the danger he was in, Paddington was sitting on a patch of ground behind the raspberry canes busy with his accounts. Mrs Bird paid him strict market

rates for all his vegetables and although she kept a careful note of all his sales Paddington wasn't the sort of bear to take chances and he liked to make doubly sure by keeping his own record. He had just finished entering the words 'MARROWS – VERRY LARGE – ONE' in his notebook when Mr Curry's voice shattered the morning air.

"Bear!" he roared. "What are you doing, bear? Resting on your laurels?"

Paddington jumped up in alarm at the sound of Mr Curry's voice. "Oh no, Mr Curry," he exclaimed, when he had recovered from the shock. "I was only sitting on my begonias."

Mr Curry looked at him suspiciously but Paddington returned his gaze very earnestly.

The cunning expression returned to Mr Curry's face as he looked round Paddington's garden. "I'm glad to see you're all up to date, bear," he said. "I was wondering if you would like to earn yourself five pence if you've a few moments to spare."

"Er... yes, please, Mr Curry," said Paddington doubtfully. From past experience he felt sure that any job for which Mr Curry was willing to pay five pence would take far longer than a few minutes, but he was much too polite to say so.

"Are you any good at climbing trees?" asked Mr Curry.

"Oh yes," said Paddington importantly. "Bears are good at climbing things."

"That's good," said Mr Curry, waving a hand in the direction of a large tree near his house. "In that case perhaps you'd like to pick a few apples for me."

"Thank you very much, Mr Curry," said Paddington, looking most surprised at the thought of being paid five pence just for picking a few apples.

"Oh, and while you're up there," said Mr Curry casually, "there's a dangerous branch that needs cutting down. I'm afraid I have to go out but it's very kind of you to offer, bear. Very kind indeed."

Before Paddington had time to open his mouth Mr Curry produced a saw and a length of rope from behind his back and pointed to the branch in question.

"Now don't forget," he said, as he handed the bits and pieces over the fence, "you tie one end of this rope to the branch, then you loop the other end over the top of the tree and tie it back down to something heavy on the ground. That's most important, otherwise the branch might fall down too quickly and cause a nasty accident. I don't want to come back and find any broken windows.

"And if you finish before I get back," continued Mr Curry, "perhaps you'd like to cut my grass. I've put the mower all ready and if you make a good job of it there might even be another five pence."

With that Mr Curry turned on his heels and disappeared in the direction of the house leaving Paddington anxiously holding the rope between his paws. He felt sure he hadn't said anything to Mr Curry about cutting down his branches, let alone uttered a word about mowing the grass. But the Browns' neighbour had a way of twisting things so that other people were never quite sure what they had said.

If it had simply been a matter of cutting the grass Paddington might have pretended that he'd got something stuck in his ear by mistake and hadn't heard properly, but as he studied Mr Curry's tree he began to look more and more thoughtful.

A few moments later he jumped up and began hurrying around as he made his preparations. Paddington like climbing trees and he was also very keen on sawing. To be able to do both at the same time seemed a very good idea indeed, especially when it was in someone else's garden.

All the same, as he looked around for something heavy to tie the rope to he soon decided that it was easier said than done. The nearest object was Mr Curry's fence and that was so rickety a piece of it came away in his paw when he tested it with one of his special knots.

In the end Paddington settled on Mr Curry's lawnmower, which looked much more solid, and after making a double knot round the handle to be on the safe side he began to climb the apple tree armed with the saw and a jar of his favourite marmalade.

Mr Curry's tree was rather old and Paddington didn't like the way it creaked, but at long last he settled himself near the branch that had to be cut down and after making sure the other end of the rope was properly tied he dipped his paw in the marmalade jar and got ready for the big moment.

Paddington was a great believer in marmalade. He'd often used it for all sorts of things besides eating, and now that he took a closer look at Mr Curry's saw he felt sure it might come in very useful for greasing the blade in an emergency. There weren't many teeth left, but of those that were still intact most were rusty and the rest stuck out at some very odd angles.

Taking a final look round to make sure everything was as it should be Paddington gripped the saw with both paws, closed his eyes, and began jumping up and down as he pushed it back and forth across the branch.

In the past he'd usually found any kind of sawing hard work, but for once everything seemed to go smoothly. If anything, Mr

Curry's tree was in an even worse state than his saw and within a few minutes of starting work there came a loud crack followed almost immediately afterwards by a splintering noise as the branch broke away from the tree.

When the shaking stopped Paddington opened his eyes and peered down at the ground. To his delight the branch was lying almost exactly where he had planned it to be and he felt very relieved as he scrambled back down the tree to view the result of his labours. It wasn't often that any jobs he did for Mr Curry went right first time and he spent some moments sitting on the sawn-off branch with a pleased expression on his face while he got his breath back.

Turning his attention to the lawn, Paddington began to wish more than ever that he hadn't heard Mr Curry's remark about cutting it. Apart from the fact that there seemed to be an awful lot, the grass itself was so long it came almost up to his knees and even when he stood up it was a job to see where the lawn finished and the rest of the garden began.

It was as he looked round for the mower in order to make some kind of a start that Paddington received his first big shock of the day. For although there was a long trail leading down through the grass from the shed, and although there were two deep wheel marks to show where it had been left standing, Mr Curry's lawnmower was no longer anywhere in sight.

Paddington's shocks never came singly, and as he nearly fell over backwards with surprise at the first one he promptly received his second.

Rubbing his eyes, he peered upwards again in the hope that it had all been part of a bad dream, but everything was exactly as it had been a few seconds before. If anything it was worse, for having rubbed his eyes he was able to make out even more clearly the awful fact that far from having disappeared into thin air Mr Curry's lawnmower was hanging as large as life from a branch high above his head.

Paddington tried pulling on the rope several times but it was much too tight to budge and after a few more half-hearted tugs he sat down again with his chin between his paws and a very disconsolate look on his face as he considered the matter.

Thinking it over he couldn't for the life of him see a way out of the problem. In fact the more he thought about it the worse it seemed, because now Mr Curry's lawnmower was up the tree he couldn't even make amends by cutting the grass for him. Mr Curry wasn't very understanding at the best of times and from whatever angle Paddington looked at the tree even he had to admit that it was one of the worst times he could remember.

"Paddington's very quiet this morning," said Mrs Brown. "I hope he's all right."

"He was poking around in Mr Brown's garage about an hour ago," said Mrs Bird. "Looking for some shears. But I haven't seen him since. If you ask me there's something going on. I met him coming up the garden path just now with a spanner in his paw and he gave me a very guilty look."

"A spanner?" said Mrs Brown. "What on earth does he want with a spanner in the garden?"

"I don't know," said Mrs Bird grimly. "But I've a nasty feeling he's got one of his ideas coming on. I know the signs."

Almost before the words were out of Mrs Bird's mouth there came a series of loud explosions from somewhere outside. "Gracious me!" she cried, as she rushed to the french windows. "There's a lot of smoke behind the raspberry canes."

"And that looks like Paddington's hat," exclaimed Mrs Brown as a shapeless looking object suddenly began bobbing up and down like a jack-in-the-box. "Perhaps he's having a bonfire. He looks as if he's trodden on something hot."

"Hmm," said Mrs Bird. "If that's a bonfire I'm a Dutchman."

Mrs Bird had had a great deal of practice at putting two and two together as far as Paddington was concerned, but before she could put her thoughts into words the banging became a roar and Paddington's hat, which had disappeared for a few seconds, suddenly shot up in the air only to hurtle along behind the top of the canes at great speed.

Any doubts in Mrs Bird's mind as to what was going on were quickly settled as Mr Brown's motor mower suddenly came into view at the end of the raspberry canes, carrying with it the familiar figure of Paddington as he held on to the handle with one paw and clutched at his hat with the other.

The mower hit Mr Curry's fence with a loud crash and then disappeared again as quickly as it had come, leaving behind it a large hole and a cloud of blue smoke.

If Mrs Brown and Mrs Bird were astonished at the strange turn of events in the garden Paddington was even more surprised. In fact so many things had happened in such a short space of time he would have been hard put to explain matters even to himself.

Mr Brown's motor mower was old and rather large and although Paddington had often watched from a safe distance when Mr Brown started it up he had never actually tried his paw at it himself.

It had all been much more difficult than he had expected and after several false starts he had almost given up hope of ever getting it to go when suddenly the engine had burst into life. One moment he'd been bending over it pulling levers and striking matches as he peered hopefully at the works, the next moment there had been a loud explosion and with no warning at all the mower had moved away of its own accord.

The next few minutes seemed like a particularly nasty nightmare. Paddington remembered going through Mr Curry's fence, and he remembered going round the lawn several times as the mower gathered speed. He

also remembered feeling very pleased that Mr
Curry had left his side gate open as he shot
through the opening and out into the road,
but after that things became so confused he
just shut his eyes and hoped for the best.

There seemed to be a lot of shouting
coming from all sides together with the sound
of running feet. Once or twice Paddington
thought he recognized the voices of Mrs
Brown and Mrs Bird in the distance, but
when he opened his eyes it was only to see a
large policeman looming up ahead.

The policeman's eyes were bulging and
he had his hand up to stop the traffic.

Paddington just had time to raise his hat as he shot past and then he found himself being whisked round a corner in the direction of the Portobello market, with the sound of a heavy pair of boots adding itself to the general hubbub.

He tried pulling on several of the levers but the more he pulled the faster he seemed to go and in no time at all the noise of his pursuers became fainter and fainter.

It felt as if he had been running for hours when suddenly, for no apparent reason, the engine began to splutter and slow down. As the motor mower came to a stop Paddington opened one eye cautiously and found to his surprise that he was standing in the middle of the Portobello Road, only a few yards away from the antique shop belonging to his friend Mr Gruber.

"Whatever's going on, Mr Brown?" cried Mr Gruber as he came running out of his shop and joined the group of street traders surrounding Paddington.

"I think I must have pulled the wrong lever by mistake, Mr Gruber," said Paddington sadly.

"Good job for you your hat fell over the carburetter," said one of the traders who knew Paddington by sight. "Otherwise there's no knowing where you'd have ended up. It must have stopped the air getting in."

"What!" exclaimed Paddington anxiously. "My hat's fallen over the carburetter?" Paddington's hat was an old and very rare one which had been given to him by his uncle shortly before he left Peru and he felt very relieved when he saw that apart from a few extra oil stains there was no sign of damage.

"If I were you," said someone in the crowd, nodding in the direction of a group of people who had just entered the market, "I should make yourself scarce. The law's on its way."

With great presence of mind Mr Gruber pushed the motor mower on to the pavement by his shop. "Quick, Mr Brown," he cried, pointing to the grass box. "Jump in here!"

Mr Gruber barely had time to cover Paddington with a sack and chalk 'Today's Bargain' on the outside of the box before there was a commotion in the crowd and the policeman elbowed his way through.

"Well," he demanded, as he withdrew a notebook from his tunic pocket and surveyed Mr Gruber. "Where is he?"

"Where is he?" repeated Mr Gruber innocently.

"The young bear that was seen driving a motor mower down the Queen's Highway a moment ago," said the policeman ponderously. "Out of control he was and heading this way."

"A young bear?" said Mr Gruber, carefully placing himself between the policeman and Mr Brown's mower. "*Driving a motor mower*. What sort of bear?"

"Dressed in a duffle coat that's seen better days," replied the policeman. "And wearing a funny kind of hat. I've seen him around before."

Mr Gruber looked about him. "I can't see anyone answering to that description," he said gravely.

The policeman stared long and hard at Mr Gruber and then at the other traders, all of whom carefully avoided catching his eye.

"I'm going for a short walk," he said at last, with the suspicion of a twinkle in his eye. "And when I get back, if I see a certain 'bargain' still outside a certain person's shop I shall make it my duty to look into the matter a bit further."

As the crowd parted to let the policeman through Mr Gruber mopped his brow. "That was a narrow squeak, Mr Brown," he whispered. "I hope I did the right thing. Not knowing the facts I didn't know quite what to say."

"That's all right, Mr Gruber," said Paddington as he peered out from under the sacking. "I'm not very sure of them myself."

Mr Gruber and the other traders listened carefully while Paddington went through the morning's events for their benefit. It took him some time to relate all that had taken place and when he'd finished Mr Gruber rubbed his chin thoughtfully.

"First things first, Mr Brown," he said briskly, as he locked the door to his shop. "It sounds as though you'll need a hand getting Mr Curry's lawnmower down from his tree before he gets home so I think I'd better push you back to Windsor Gardens as quickly as possible. Unless, of course, you'd rather walk?"

Paddington sat up in the grass box for a moment while he considered the matter. "I think if you don't mind, Mr Gruber," he announced gratefully, as he pulled the sack back over his head, "I'd much rather ride."

Apart from not wishing to see Mr Curry or the policeman again that morning, Paddington had a nasty feeling Mrs Brown and Mrs Bird must be somewhere around and he didn't want to delay matters any further by going all through his explanations once again before he'd had time to think them out properly.

In fact, all in all, Paddington was only too pleased to have the chance of a comfortable ride home in the dark and safety of a boxful of grass clippings, especially as he'd just discovered the remains of a marmalade sandwich which he'd fastened to the inside of his hat with a piece of sticky tape for just such an emergency.

Chapter Two

Mr Gruber's Outing

Most mornings when he wasn't busy in the garden Paddington visited his friend Mr Gruber, and the day after his adventure with the motor mower he made his way in the direction of the Portobello Road even earlier than usual.

He was particularly anxious not to see Mr Curry for a few days and he agreed with Mrs Bird when she said at breakfast that it was better to let sleeping dogs lie.

Not that Mr Curry showed much sign of sleeping. From quite an early hour he'd been on the prowl, peering at the hole in his fence in the intervals between glaring across at the Browns' house, and Paddington cast several anxious glances over his shoulder as he hurried down Windsor Gardens pushing his shopping basket on wheels. He heaved a sigh of relief when he at last found himself safely inside Mr Gruber's shop among all the familiar antiques and copper pots and pans.

Apart from a few grass cuttings stuck to his fur Paddington was none the worse for his adventure, and while Mr Gruber made the cocoa for their elevenses he sat on the horsehair sofa at the back of the shop and sorted through the morning supply of buns.

Mr Gruber chuckled as they went over the previous day's happenings together while they sipped their cocoa. "Hearing about other people's adventures always makes me restless, Mr Brown," he said, as he looked out of his window at the bright morning sun. "Particularly when it's a nice day. I've a good mind to shut up shop after lunch and take the afternoon off."

Mr Gruber coughed. "I wonder if you would care to accompany me, Mr Brown," he said. "We could go for a stroll in the park and look at some of the sights."

"Ooh, yes, please, Mr Gruber," exclaimed Paddington. "I should like that very much." Paddington enjoyed going out with Mr Gruber for he knew a great deal about London and he always made things seem interesting.

"We could take Jonathan and Judy," said Mr Gruber, "and make a picnic of it."

Mr Gruber became more and more enthusiastic as he thought the matter over. "All work and no play never did anyone any good, Mr Brown," he said. "And it's a long time since I had an outing."

With that he began to bustle round his shop tidying things up and he even announced that he wouldn't be putting his 'knick-knacks' table outside that day, which was most unusual, for Mr Gruber always had a table on the pavement outside his shop laden with curios and knick-knacks of all kinds at bargain prices.

While Mr Gruber busied himself at the back of the shop Paddington spent the time drawing out a special notice in red ink to hang on the shop door while they were away. It said:

IMMPORTANT AN – OUNCEMENT
THIS SHOP WILL BE CLOSED FOR THE ANNULE
STAFF OUTING THIS AFTERNOON!!!!

After underlining the words with the remains of the cocoa lumps Paddington carefully wiped his paws and then waved

to Mr Gruber before hurrying off to
the morning shopping.

When she heard the news of the
forthcoming outing Mrs Bird quickly entered
into the spirit of things and she made a great
pile of sandwiches – ham and two kinds
of jam for Mr Gruber, Jonathan, and Judy,
and some special marmalade ones for
Paddington.

These, together with a tin of freshly made
fairy cakes and some bottles of lemonade soon
filled Jonathan's rucksack to the brim.

"Sooner Mr Gruber than me," said Mrs
Bird after lunch as she watched the heavily
laden party set off up the road led by Mr
Gruber carrying a large guidebook and
Paddington with his suitcase, opera glasses,
and a pile of maps.

"Paddington did say they're going to the
park, didn't he?" asked Mrs Brown. "It looks
rather as if they're off to the North Pole."

"Knowing Paddington," said Mrs Bird
darkly, "perhaps it's as well they're prepared
for any emergency!"

In Mrs Bird's experience an outing with
Paddington was more likely than not to end
up in some kind of disaster and she wasn't
sorry to be out of the way for a change.

All the same Mrs Bird would have been hard put to find fault with the orderly procession which neared the park some while later, and even the policeman on point duty nodded approvingly when Mr Gruber signalled that they wanted to cross the road. He at once held up the traffic with one hand and touched his helmet with the other when Paddington raised his hat as they went by.

It had taken them quite a long time to reach the park for there had been a great many shop windows to look in on the way, and Mr Gruber had stopped several times in order to point out some interesting sights he didn't want them to miss.

Although Paddington had been in a number of parks before, it was the first time

in his life he had ever seen a really big one and as Mr Gruber led the way through the big iron gates he decided he was going to enjoy himself. Apart from the grass and trees there were fountains, swings, deck chairs, and in the distance he could even see a lake shimmering in the afternoon sun. In fact there was so much to see he had to blink several times in order to make sure he was still in London.

Mr Gruber beamed with pleasure at the look on Paddington's face. "It might be an idea to go and sit by the lake first of all, Mr Brown," he said. "Then you can dip your paws in the water to cool off while we have our sandwiches."

"Thank you very much, Mr Gruber," said Paddington gratefully. The hot pavements always made his feet tired and the thought of being able to cool them and have a marmalade sandwich at the same time seemed a very good idea.

For the next few minutes Mr Gruber's party was very quiet indeed and the only sound apart from the distant roar of the traffic was an occasional splash as Paddington dipped his paws in the water and the clink of a marmalade jar as he made some extra sandwiches to be on the safe side.

When they had finished their picnic Mr Gruber led the way towards a small enclosure where the swings and slides were kept and he stood back while Paddington, Jonathan, and Judy hurried inside to see what they could find. Paddington in particular was very keen on slides and he was anxious to test a large one which he had seen from a distance.

It was when the excitement was at its height that Mr Gruber suddenly cupped one hand to his ear and called for quiet.

"I do believe there's a band playing somewhere," he said.

Sure enough, as the others listened they could definitely hear strains of music floating across the park. It seemed to be coming from behind a clump of trees and as Mr Gruber led the way across the park it gradually got louder and louder.

Then, as they rounded a corner, another large enclosure came into view. At one end of it there was a bandstand and in front of that there were rows and rows of seats filled with people listening to the music.

Mr Gruber pointed excitedly at the bandstand. "We're in luck, Mr Brown," he exclaimed. "It's the Guards!"

While Mr Gruber went on to explain

that the Guards were a very famous regiment of soldiers who kept watch over Buckingham Palace and other important places, Paddington peered through the fence at the men on the platform. They all wore brightly coloured uniforms with very tall black hats made of fur and their instruments were so highly polished they sparkled in the sun like balls of fire.

"It's a good many years since I went to a band concert in the park, Mr Brown," said Mr Gruber.

"I've *never* been to one, Mr Gruber," said Paddington.

"That settles it then," replied Mr Gruber. And as the item came to an end and the audience applauded he led the way to the entrance and asked for four five pence tickets. They just managed to squeeze themselves into four seats near the back before the conductor,

a very imposing man with a large moustache, raised his baton for the next item.

Paddington settled himself comfortably in his seat. They had done so much walking that day he wasn't at all sorry to be able to sit down and rest his paws for a while and he applauded dutifully and cheered several times when, with a flourish, the conductor at last brought the music to an end and turned to salute the audience.

Judy nudged Paddington. "You can see what they're going to play next," she whispered, pointing towards the bandstand. "It's written on that board up there."

Paddington took out his opera glasses and leaned out into the aisle as he peered at the board with interest. There were several items called 'Selections' which he didn't immediately recognize. These were followed by a number of regimental marches, one of which had just been played. After that came another selection from something called a 'Surprise Symphony', which sounded very good value.

But it was as he peered at the last item that a strange expression suddenly came over Paddington's face. He breathed heavily on his glasses several times, polished them with a piece of rag which he got from his suitcase, and then looked through them again at the board.

"That's called a selection from Schubert's Unfinished Symphony," explained Judy in a whisper as the music started up again.

"What!" exclaimed Paddington hotly as his worst suspicions were confirmed. "Mr Gruber's paid five pence each for our tickets and they haven't even finished it!"

"He died a long time ago," whispered Judy, "and they never found the rest of it."

"Five pence each!" exclaimed Paddington bitterly, not listening to Judy's words. "That's twenty pence!"

"Ssh!" said someone in the row behind.

Paddington sank back into his seat and spent the next few minutes giving the conductor some hard stares through his opera glasses.

Gradually, as the music reached a quiet passage, everyone closed their eyes and began to sink lower and lower in their seats until within a matter of moments the only movement came from somewhere near the back of the audience as a small brown figure got up from its seat by the gangway and crept towards the exit.

Paddington felt very upset about the matter of the Unfinished Symphony, particularly as it was Mr Gruber's treat, and he was determined to investigate the matter.

"'Ere," said the man at the entrance. "If you goes out you won't be allowed in again. It's against the rules and regulations."

Paddington raised his hat. "I'd like to see Mr Schubert, please," he explained.

"Sherbet?" repeated the man. He cupped one hand to his ear. The band had reached a loud passage and it was difficult to hear what Paddington was saying. "You'd better try over there," he exclaimed, pointing to a small kiosk. "I believe they 'as some dabs."

"Dabs?" exclaimed Paddington, looking most surprised.

"That's right," said the man. "But you'll 'ave to look slippy," he called as Paddington hurried across the grass with an anxious expression on his face. "Otherwise I shall have to charge you another five pence."

The lady in the kiosk looked rather startled when Paddington tapped on the side. "Oh dear," she said, as she peered over the counter. "One of them soldiers has dropped his busby."

"I'm not a busby!" exclaimed Paddington

hotly. "I'm a bear and I've come to see Mr Schubert."

"Mr *Schubert*?" repeated the lady, recovering from her shock. "I don't know anyone of that name, dear. There's a Bert what sees to the deck chairs but it's his day off today."

She turned to another lady at the back. "Do you know a Mr Schubert, Glad?" she queried. "There's a young bear gentleman asking after him."

"Sounds like one of them musicians," said the second lady doubtfully. "They usually 'as fancy names."

"He wrote a symphony," explained Paddington. "And he forgot to finish it."

"Oh dear," said the first lady. "Well, if I were you I'd go and wait under that bandstand. You're bound to catch them when they come off then."

"There's a door at the back," she added helpfully. "If you wait in there it'll save disturbing all the people in the audience."

After thanking the ladies for all their help Paddington hurried back across the grass towards some steps which led down to a small door marked STRICTLY PRIVATE at the rear of the bandstand.

Paddington liked anything new and he'd never been inside a bandstand before. It sounded most interesting and he was looking forward to investigating the matter.

The door opened easily when he put his paw against it but it was when he closed it behind him that he made the first of several nasty discoveries, for it shut with an ominous click and try as he might he couldn't pull it open again.

After poking at it for several minutes with an old broom handle which he found on the floor Paddington groped around until he found an upturned box and then he sat down in order to consider the matter.

Apart from the fact that it was dark inside the bandstand it was also very dusty and every time the band played a loud passage a shower of dust floated down and landed on his whiskers making him sneeze. In fact the more Paddington thought about things the less he liked the look of them, and the less he liked the look of things the more he thought something would have to be done.

"Oh dear," groaned Judy. "I've never known such a bear for disappearing."

Mr Gruber, Jonathan, and Judy had

opened their eyes at the end of the piece of music only to discover that Paddington's chair was empty and he was nowhere in sight.

"He's left his fairy cakes behind," said Jonathan, "so he can't have gone far."

Mr Gruber looked worried. "They're just about to play the 'Surprise Symphony'," he said. "I do hope he's back in time for that." Mr Gruber knew how keen Paddington was on surprises and he felt sure he would enjoy the item.

But before they had time to discuss the matter any further the conductor brought the band to attention with a wave of his baton and quiet descended on the audience once again.

It was when the band had been playing for about five minutes that a puzzled look

gradually came over Mr Gruber's face. "It seems a very unusual version," he whispered to Jonathan and Judy. "I've never heard it played like this before."

Now that Mr Gruber mentioned it there did seem to be something odd about the music. Other people in the audience were beginning to notice it as well and even the conductor was twirling his moustache with a worried expression on his face. It wasn't so much the way the music was being played as a strange thumping noise which seemed to be coming from the bandstand itself and which seemed to be getting louder every minute.

Several times the conductor glared at the man who was playing the drums until at last, looking most upset, the man raised his sticks in the air to show that he had nothing to do with the matter.

It was at that moment that an even stranger thing happened. One moment the conductor was standing in front of the band glaring at the musicians, the next moment there was a splintering noise and before everyone's astonished gaze he appeared to rise several inches into the air before he toppled over clutching at the rail behind him.

"Crikey!" exclaimed Jonathan as a loud sneeze broke the silence that followed. "I'd know that sneeze anywhere!"

Mr Gruber, Jonathan, and Judy watched with growing alarm as a board in the floor of the bandstand gradually rose higher and higher and after some more splintering noises a broom handle came into view and waved about in the air. A few seconds later the broom handle was followed by a familiar-looking hat and some even more familiar-looking whiskers.

"Excuse me," said Paddington, raising his hat politely to the conductor. "I'm looking for Mr Schubert."

"Bears in my bandstand!" spluttered the conductor. "Thirty years I've been conducting and never once fallen off my podium, let alone been knocked off by a bear!"

Whatever else the conductor had been about to say was drowned in a burst of applause. First one person started to clap, then another, until finally the whole audience was on its feet applauding. Several people shouted "Bravo!" and a number of others echoed it with cries of "Encore!"

"They call it the 'Surprise Symphony'," said a man sitting next to Mr Gruber, "but I don't think I've ever been more surprised in my life as when that young bear came up through the floor."

"Very good value for five pence," said someone else. "What will they think of next?"

It was some while before the applause died down and by that time the conductor had recovered himself and he even began to look quite pleased at the way the audience was clapping.

"Very good timing, bear," he said gruffly as he returned Paddington to his seat and gave him a smart military salute. "It would have done credit to a Guardsman."

"All the same," said Jonathan some while later as they were strolling home through the park, "it's a jolly good thing someone started the clapping off or there's no knowing what might have happened. I wonder who it was?"

Judy looked at Mr Gruber but he appeared to be examining one of the nearby trees and if there was a twinkle in his eye it was hard to see. In any case, before they had time to discuss the matter any further the quiet of the afternoon was broken by the sound of music and marching feet.

"It must be the band on their way back to the barracks," said Mr Gruber. "If we hurry we may be in time to see them." So saying he quickly led the way in the direction of the music until they reached the side of the road just as a long line of soldiers came swinging into view led by the officer in charge.

"I'm glad you've seen the Guards marching, Mr Brown," said Mr Gruber some moments later as the music died away and the last of the soldiers disappeared from view. "It's a lovely sight."

Paddington nodded his agreement as he replaced his hat. He'd been most impressed by the sight and although when they'd passed by the soldiers had all been staring very smartly straight ahead he was almost sure the man in charge had turned his eyes in their direction for a fraction of a second.

"I had a feeling he did too, Mr Brown," said Mr Gruber when Paddington mentioned it. "And I should certainly make a note of it in your scrap book. I don't suppose it'll ever happen again and it's a very good way to round off a most enjoyable day."

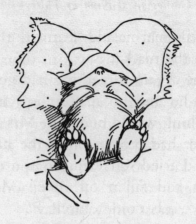

Chapter Three

GOINGS ON AT
NUMBER THIRTY-TWO

Paddington woke with a start and then sat up in bed rubbing his eyes. For a moment or two he wasn't quite sure where he was but gradually, as a number of familiar objects swam into view, he realized with surprise that he was in his own room.

The afternoon sun was streaming in through the window and after blinking several times he lay back again with his paws behind his head and a thoughtful expression on his face.

Although he wasn't quite sure what had disturbed him he felt very glad he'd woken when he did for he had been in the middle of a particularly nasty dream about a large jar of his special marmalade from the cut-price grocer in the market.

In the dream something had gone wrong with the lid and no matter how much he'd tried nothing would budge it. Mrs Bird's best tin opener had broken off at the handle, and when he'd tried squeezing it in a door jamb the door had fallen off. Even Mr Brown's hammer and cold chisel had made no impression at all and after several bangs the head had flown off the hammer and broken the dining-room window. In fact, if he hadn't woken at that moment there was no knowing what other awful things might have happened.

Paddington heaved a sigh of relief and, after dipping a paw into an open jar of marmalade by his bed in order to make sure everything really was all right, he closed his eyes again.

The Brown household was unusually quiet and peaceful that afternoon for Paddington had the house to himself. In the morning the postman had brought Jonathan and Judy a surprise invitation to a tea party and by the same delivery a letter had arrived asking Mrs Brown and Mrs Bird to visit an old Aunt who lived on the other side of London.

Even Paddington should have been out, for Mr Brown had given him several books to take back to the Public Library together with a long list of things he wanted looking up in the Reference department.

It was Mr Brown's list which had proved to be Paddington's undoing for he had taken it upstairs to his room after lunch in order to study it and before he knew where he was he had nodded off.

Thinking the matter over Paddington wasn't quite sure whether it was the result of an extra large lunch, with two helpings of suet pudding, or the hot afternoon sun, or even a mixture of both; but whatever the reason he must have been asleep for over an hour for in the distance he could hear a clock striking three.

It was as the last of the chimes died away that Paddington suddenly sat bolt upright in his bed and stared with wide open eyes at the ceiling. Unless he was dreaming again there was a strange scraping noise coming from somewhere directly overhead. It began by the door, then passed across the room in the direction of the window and paused for a moment before coming all the way back again.

Paddington's eyes got larger and larger as he listened to the sound, and they nearly popped out altogether a few moments later when a noise remarkably like that of a hammer and chisel broke the silence which followed the scraping.

After pinching himself several times to make sure it had nothing to do with his dream Paddington jumped out of bed and hurried across the room in order to investigate the matter.

As he flung open the window an even stranger thing happened and he jumped back into the room as if he had been shot, for just as he peered outside a long black snake-like object came into view and hung there twisting and turning for several seconds before it finally disappeared from view below the ledge.

Paddington backed across the room and after making a grab for his hat and suitcase, rushed out on to the landing, banging the door behind him.

Although after the dream and the strange events that had followed he was prepared for almost anything Paddington certainly wasn't expecting the sight which met his eyes on the landing and he almost wished he'd stayed in his room.

Only a few yards away, between his door and the top of the stairs, there was a ladder which definitely hadn't been there after lunch. It was leaning against the trap door in the ceiling and worse still the trap door itself was wide open.

Paddington was a brave bear at heart but even so it took him several moments to pluck up his courage again. After pulling his hat well down over his head and carefully placing his suitcase at the top of the stairs in case of an emergency, he began climbing slowly up the ladder.

It was when he reached the top rung and peered over the edge into the loft that Paddington's worst suspicions were realized. For there, tip-toeing across the rafters with a torch in one hand and what looked like a long knife in the other, was a man in a trilby hat and blue overalls.

Holding his breath Paddington considered the matter for several seconds before coming to a decision. As quietly as possible, he stretched his paw into the darkness until he felt the edge of the trap door and then he flung it back into place and pushed the bolt home as hard as he could before scrambling down the ladder on to the landing and safety.

All at once there was a commotion in the roof as someone started to shout, then several bumps, followed by the sound of banging on the other side of the trap door. But by that time Paddington was much too far away to hear what was going on. The sound of the Browns' front door slamming had added itself to the general hubbub and he was halfway down Windsor Gardens, hurrying along the pavement with a very determined expression on his face indeed. All in all, he decided that bad though his dream had been, things had been even worse since he'd woken up and it was definitely time to call for help.

After rounding several corners Paddington at last reached the place he had been looking for. It was a large, old-fashioned stone building which stood slightly apart from the rest on a corner site. Most of the windows had bars across them and at the top of some steps leading up to the entrance there was a blue lamp with the word POLICE written across it in white letters.

Paddington hurried up the steps and then paused at the entrance. Leading from the hall there were a number of doors and it was difficult to decide which was the best one. In the end he picked on a large brown door on his right. It looked more important than any of the others and Paddington was a firm believer in going to the top whenever he had an emergency.

After knocking several times he waited with his ear against the keyhole until he heard a gruff voice call out "Come in" and then he pushed the door open with his paw.

The only person in the room was a man sitting behind a desk near the window and he looked rather cross when he saw Paddington. "You've come to the wrong place," he said. "Undesirables are supposed to report round the back."

"*Undesirables!*" exclaimed Paddington hotly, giving the man a hard stare. "I'm not an undesirable. I'm a bear!"

The man jumped up from behind his desk. "I beg your pardon," he said. "The light's none too good and I thought for a moment you were Hairy Harry."

"*Hairy Harry?*" repeated Paddington, hardly able to believe his ears.

"He's what we call the 'Portobello Prowler'," the man added confidentially, "and he's been giving us a lot of trouble lately. He's only small and he slips in through pantry windows when no one's looking."

His voice trailed away as Paddington's

stare got harder and harder. "Er… what can we do for you?" he asked.

"I'd like to see Sid, please," said Paddington, putting down his suitcase.

"Sid?" repeated the man looking most surprised. "I don't think we have any Sids here. We've several Alfs and a Bert, but I don't recall any Sids off hand."

"It says on the notice outside you've got one," said Paddington firmly. "It's written on the door."

The man looked puzzled for a moment and then his face cleared. "You don't mean *Sid* – you mean C.I.D.

"That's quite a different matter," he explained. "C.I.D. stands for Criminal Investigation Department."

"Well, there's a criminal in Mr Brown's roof," said Paddington, not to be outdone. "And I think he needs investigating."

"A criminal in Mr Brown's roof?" repeated the man, taking a notepad and pencil as he listened while Paddington went on to explain all that had taken place.

"Good work, bear," he exclaimed when Paddington had finished talking. "We don't often catch anyone red-handed. I'll send out an alert at once."

With that he pressed a button on the side of his desk and in a matter of seconds the Police Station became a hive of activity. In fact Paddington hardly had time to adjust his hat and pick up his suitcase before he found himself being led by several policemen into a yard at the back of the building where he was bundled into the back seat of a large black car.

Paddington felt most important as the car shot down the road in the direction of Windsor Gardens. He had never been inside a police car before and it was all very interesting. He didn't remember ever having travelled quite as fast either, and he was most impressed when a policeman on point duty held up all the other traffic and waved them across some lights which were at red.

"Right, bear," said the C.I.D. man as the car screeched to a halt outside the Browns' house, "lead the way. Only watch out – if he's got a knife he may be dangerous."

Paddington thought for a moment and then raised his hat. "After you," he said politely. Taking things all round Paddington felt he'd had his share of adventures for one day and apart from that he was anxious to make sure his store of marmalade was safe before anything else happened.

"Do you mean to say," exclaimed the policeman as he looked down at the man in the blue overalls, "you were putting up a television aerial all the time?"

"That's right, officer," said the man. "And I've got a letter from Mr Brown to prove it. Gave me the key of the house he did. Said there would be no one else here as he was getting rid of them for the day and I was to let myself in on account of it being a special surprise for the rest of the family and he didn't want them to know about it."

The man in the overalls paused for breath and then handed a card to the policeman. "Higgins is the name. Tip Top Tellys. If you ever want a job done just give me a ring."

"Tip Top Tellys?" repeated the C.I.D. man, looking distastefully at the card. He turned to Paddington. "I thought you said he had a knife, bear?"

"That wasn't a knife," said Mr Higgins. "That was my tweeker."

"Your *tweeker*!" exclaimed Paddington, looking most upset.

"That's right," said Mr Higgins cheerfully, as he held up a long screwdriver. "Always carry one of these on account of having to give the old tellies a tweek when they want adjusting.

"Tell you what," he added, as he waved his hand in the direction of a large cabinet which stood in one corner of the dining-room, "I'm nearly ready to switch on. Just got to connect the aerial. With this young bear's permission, I vote we take five minutes off and brew up a cup of tea. There's nothing like a nice cup of tea for cooling things down."

Mr Higgins gave Paddington a broad wink. "If there's a detective play on we might even pick up a few hints!"

As a spluttering noise came from one of the policemen Paddington disappeared hurriedly in the direction of the kitchen. The C.I.D. man's face seemed to have gone a rather nasty shade of red, and he didn't like the look of it at all.

All the same, when he returned a few minutes later staggering under the weight of a tray full of cups and saucers and a large plate of buns even the policemen began to look more cheerful, and in no time at all the dining-room began to echo with the sound of laughter as everyone recounted their part in the afternoon's adventure.

In between explaining all about the various knobs on the television and making some last minute adjustments Mr Higgins kept them all amused with tales of other adventures he'd had in the trade. In fact the time passed so quickly everyone seemed sorry when at last it was time to leave.

"I've just sold two more television sets," whispered Mr Higgins, nodding towards the policemen as he paused at the door. "So if I can ever do you a favour just let me know. One good turn deserves another."

"Thank you very much, Mr Higgins," said Paddington gratefully.

Having waved goodbye to everyone Paddington shut the front door and hurried back into the dining-room. Although he was pleased that the mystery of the bumps in the roof had been solved he was anxious to test Mr Brown's new television set before the others arrived home and he quickly drew the curtains before settling himself comfortably in one of the armchairs.

In the past he had often watched television in a shop window in the Portobello Road, but the manager had several times come out to complain about his breathing heavily on the windows during the cowboy films and Paddington was sure it would be much nicer to be able to sit at home and watch in comfort.

But when he had seen a cartoon, some cricket, two musical items, and a programme on bird watching, Paddington's interest began to flag and after helping himself to another bun he turned his attention to a small booklet which Mr Higgins had left behind.

The book was called 'How to Get the

Best Out of Your Television' and it was full of pictures and diagrams – rather like maps of the Underground – showing the inside of the set. There was even a chapter showing how to adjust the various knobs in order to get the best pictures and Paddington spent some time sitting in front of the set turning the brightness up and down and making unusual patterns on the screen.

There were so many different knobs to turn and so many different things it was possible to do with the picture that he soon lost all account of the time and he was most surprised when the dining-room clock suddenly struck six.

It was while he was hurriedly turning all the knobs back to where they'd been to start with that something very unexpected and alarming happened.

One moment a cowboy on a white horse was dashing across the screen in hot pursuit of a man with a black moustache and side-whiskers, the next moment there was a click and before Paddington's astonished gaze the picture shrank in size until there was nothing left but a small white dot.

He spent some moments peering hopefully at the screen through his opera glasses, but the longer he looked the smaller the dot became and even striking a match didn't help matters for by the time he had been in the kitchen to fetch the box the spot had disappeared completely.

Paddington stood in front of the silent receiver with a mournful expression on his face. Although Mr Brown had gone to a lot of trouble in order to surprise the family it was quite certain he wouldn't be at all pleased if they received that much of a surprise and arrived home to find it wasn't even working.

Paddington heaved a deep sigh. "Oh dear," he said, as he addressed the world in general. "I'm in trouble again."

"I can't understand it," said Mr Brown as he came out of the dining-room. "Mr Higgins promised faithfully it would be all ready by the time we got home."

"Never mind, Henry," said Mrs Brown as the rest of the family crowded round the doorway. "It was a surprise and I'm sure he'll be able to get it working soon."

"Crikey!" exclaimed Jonathan. "He must have been having a lot of trouble. Look at all the pieces."

"Don't bother to draw the curtains. We'll eat in the kitchen," said Mrs Brown as she took in the scene. There were bits and pieces everywhere, not to mention a large number of valves and a cathode ray tube on the settee.

Mrs Bird looked puzzled. "I thought you said it wasn't working," she remarked.

"I don't see how it could be," replied Mr Brown.

"Well, there's something there," said Mrs Bird, pointing to the screen. "I saw it move."

The Brown family peered through the gloom at the television set. Although it didn't seem possible Mrs Bird could be right, now they looked there was definitely some kind of movement on the glass.

"It looks rather furry," said Mrs Brown. "Perhaps it's one of those animal programmes. They do have a lot on television."

Jonathan was nearest to the screen and he suddenly clutched Judy's arm. "Crumbs!" he whispered, as his eyes grew accustomed to the dark and he caught sight of a familiar-looking nose pressed against the glass. "It isn't a programme. It's Paddington. He must be stuck inside the cabinet!"

"This is most interesting," said Mr Brown, taking out his glasses. "Switch on the light someone. I'd like a closer look."

As a muffled exclamation came from somewhere inside the television Jonathan and Judy hurriedly placed themselves between Mr Brown and the screen.

"Don't you think you ought to ring Mr Higgins, Dad?" asked Judy. "He'll know what to do."

"We'll go down and fetch him if you like," said Jonathan eagerly. "It won't take a minute."

"Yes, come along, Henry," said Mrs Brown. "I should leave things just as they are. There's no knowing what might happen if you touch them."

Rather reluctantly Mr Brown allowed himself to be shepherded out of the room closely followed by Jonathan and Judy.

Mrs Bird was the last one to leave and before she closed the door she took one last look round the room. "There are some rather nasty marmalade stains on that cabinet," she said in a loud voice. "If I were a young bear I'd make sure they're wiped off by the time Mr Higgins gets here... otherwise certain people may put two and two together."

Although Mrs Bird kept a firm hand on 'goings on' in the Brown household she was a great believer in the proverb 'least said – soonest mended,' especially when it had to do with anything as complicated as a television set.

If Mr Higgins was surprised at having to repay Paddington's good turn so soon he didn't show it by so much as the flicker of an eyelid. All the same, after Mrs Bird had spoken to him he took Paddington on one side and they had a long chat together while he explained how dangerous it was to take the back off a television receiver if you didn't know what you were doing.

"It's a good job bears' paws are well insulated, Mr Brown," he said as he bade goodbye to Paddington. "Otherwise you might not be here to tell the tale."

"That's all right," he added cheerfully, as Paddington thanked him for all his trouble. "Got a bit of marmalade on my tweeker, but otherwise there's no harm done. And I daresay it'll wash off."

"It usually does," said Mrs Bird with the voice of experience, as she showed him to the door.

As the Browns trooped into the dining-room for their first evening's viewing it was noticeable that one member of the family settled himself as far away from the screen as possible. Although Mr Higgins had screwed the back on the television as tightly as his tweeker would allow, Paddington wasn't taking any more chances than he could help.

"Mind you," said Mr Brown, later that evening when Mrs Bird came in with the bedtime snack, "I still can't understand what it was we saw on the screen. It was very strange."

"It was probably some kind of interference," said Mrs Bird gravely. "I don't suppose it'll happen again, do you Paddington?"

As she spoke several pairs of eyes turned in Paddington's direction but most of his face was carefully hidden behind a large mug and very wisely he only nodded his agreement. Not that he was having to pretend he felt tired for in fact it was only the cocoa steam that was keeping his eyelids open at all. Nevertheless, there was something about the way his whiskers were poking out on either side of the mug that suggested Mrs Bird had hit the nail on the head and that as far as the Brown family were concerned there was one kind of interference they weren't likely to get on their television again in a hurry.

Chapter Four

PADDINGTON HITS THE JACKPOT

"'Lucky For Some'?" exclaimed Mr Brown. "Don't tell me we've got to sit and watch that awful thing. Isn't there anything better on the other channel?"

The rest of the family exchanged uneasy glances. "Paddington did ask if we could have it on," said Mrs Brown. "It's his favourite programme and he seemed particularly anxious we shouldn't miss it tonight."

"In that case," said Mr Brown, "why isn't he here?"

"I expect he's popped out somewhere," said Mrs Brown soothingly. "He'll probably be back in a minute."

Mr Brown sank back into his seat with a grunt and stared distastefully at the television screen as a fanfare of trumpets heralded the start of 'Lucky For Some' and the Master of Ceremonies, Ronnie Playfair, came bounding on to the stage rubbing his hands with glee.

"I wouldn't mind," said Mr Brown, "if he asked sensible questions. But to give all that money away for the sort of things he asks is ridiculous."

The dining-room curtains were drawn and the Brown family, with the exception of Paddington, who had been unaccountably missing since shortly after tea, were settled in a small half-circle facing the television set in preparation for their evening's viewing.

Over the past few weeks a change had come over the routine at number thirty-two Windsor Gardens. Normally the Browns were the sort of family who entertained themselves quite happily, but since the arrival of the television set practically every evening had been spent in semi-darkness as they sat with their eyes glued to the screen.

All the same, although Mr Brown was the first to admit it out loud, the nine days' wonder of having pictures in their own home was beginning to wear thin and there were several signs of restlessness as yet another fanfare of trumpets burst from the loudspeaker.

"I do hope nothing's happened to Paddington," whispered Mrs Brown. "It's not like him to miss any of the programmes, especially a quiz. He's very keen on them."

"That bear's been acting strangely all week," said Mrs Bird. "Ever since he got that letter. I've a nasty feeling it may have something to do with it."

"Well, it can't be anything bad," said Mrs Brown. "He seems to have spent all his time with his whiskers buried in those encyclopaedias of Mr Gruber's. He even missed his second helping at lunch today."

"That's just it," said Mrs Bird ominously. "It's much too good to be true."

While Ronnie Playfair's face grew larger and larger on the screen as he explained the programme to the studio audience and the viewers at home, the Browns began to discuss Paddington's strange behaviour over the past week.

As Mr Bird said it had all begun when he'd received an important-looking letter by the first post one morning. At the time no one had paid it a great deal of attention for he often sent away for catalogues or any free samples which he saw being advertised in the newspapers.

But a little later that same morning he had arrived home pushing Mr Gruber's encyclopaedias in his basket on wheels and the next day, after borrowing Mr Brown's library tickets, another pile of books had added themselves to the already large one at his bedside.

"He's been asking the oddest questions too," said Mrs Brown. "I don't know where he gets them from."

"Well, wherever it is," said Mr Brown, as he looked up from his evening paper, "I hope he gets back soon."

Mr Brown liked plays and had just discovered there was a particularly good one about to start on the other channel.

"Crikey!" exclaimed Jonathan suddenly, as he jumped up from his seat and pointed at the television screen. "No wonder he isn't here! Look!"

"Gracious me!" exclaimed Mrs Bird as she followed his gaze. "It can't be!"

Mr Brown adjusted his glasses. "It jolly well is," he said. "It's Paddington and Mr Gruber."

While the Browns had been talking Ronnie Playfair had finished describing the workings of the programme. Waving his hand cheerily to the studio audience he stepped down off the stage in the beam of a large spotlight and announced that the first contestant of the evening was a Mr Brown of London.

As he made his way up the aisle the camera followed him and eventually came to rest on two familiar faces at the end of one of the rows of seats. Mr Gruber's look of embarrassment was tinged with a faint air of guilt as he caught sight of his own face on a nearby screen. Although Paddington had assured him that the Browns liked surprises he wasn't at all sure they would be keen on this particular one.

But Mr Gruber was soon lost from view as a small brown figure sitting next to him raised a battered hat to the camera and hurried up the aisle after the Master of Ceremonies.

If the Browns were overcome at the sight of Paddington climbing on to the stage Ronnie Playfair was equally at a loss for words, which was most unusual.

"Are you sure you're the right Mr Brown?" he asked nervously, as Paddington dumped his suitcase on the stage and raised his hat to the audience.

"Yes, Mr Playfair," said Paddington, waving a piece of paper importantly in the air. "I've got your letter asking me to come."

"I… er… I didn't know there were any bears in Notting Hill Gate," said Ronnie Playfair.

"I *come* from Peru," said Paddington. "But I *live* in Windsor Gardens."

"Oh well," said Ronnie Playfair, recovering himself slightly, "we won't ask you to *peruve* that, but I suppose we must expect the *bear* facts tonight.

"*Peruve* that," he repeated, laughing at his own joke in a rather high voice. "*Bear* facts." His voice died away as he caught Paddington's eye. Paddington didn't think much of Ronnie Playfair's jokes and he was giving him a particularly hard stare.

"Er… perhaps you'd like to step forward and send a message home," said the Master of

Ceremonies hurriedly. "We always ask our contestants to send a message home – it makes them feel at ease."

Paddington bent down and took a piece of paper out of his suitcase. "Thank you very much, Mr Playfair," he exclaimed, as he began advancing on the camera.

The Browns watched in dumb fascination as Paddington loomed larger on their screen. "Hullo all at number thirty-two," said a familiar voice. "I hope I shan't be late, Mrs Bird. Mr Gruber promised to bring me straight home and…"

Whatever else Paddington had been about to say was lost as there came a loud crash and the picture disappeared from the screen.

"Oh no," cried Judy. "Don't say it's broken down. Not tonight of all nights."

"It's all right," said Jonathan. "Look — they've got another camera on."

As he spoke another picture flashed on to the screen. It wasn't quite such a nice one as the close-up of Paddington had been. Until just before the end, when it had suddenly gone soft and muzzy, that one had shown almost every whisker, whereas the new picture was looking towards the audience and there appeared to be some confusion. One of the cameramen was sitting on the floor surrounded by wires and cables, rubbing his head; and Ronnie Playfair seemed to be having some kind of an argument with a man wearing headphones.

"He wasn't on his marks," cried the cameraman. "He kept following me. You can't take proper close-ups if people don't stay on their marks."

Paddington peered at the floor. "My marks?" he repeated hotly. "But I had a bath before I came out."

"He doesn't mean *dirt* marks," said Ronnie Playfair, pointing to a yellow chalk line. "He means that sort. You're supposed to stay where I put you otherwise the cameras can't get their shots."

"You did ask me to step forward," said Paddington, looking most upset.

"I said *step* forward," said Ronnie Playfair crossly, "Not go for a walk."

Ronnie Playfair had been Master of Ceremonies on 'Lucky For Some' for several years with never a word out of place, let alone an upset like the one that had just occurred, and there was a strained look on his face as he picked his way back across the cables closely followed by Paddington who was peering anxiously at the floor in case he lost sight of his chalk mark again.

"Now," he said, as they reached the centre of the stage and stood facing the other cameras, "what would you like to be questioned on?" He waved his hand in the direction of four barrels which stood in a row on a nearby table. "You can have History, Geography, Mathematics, or General Knowledge."

Paddington thought for a moment. "I think I'd like to try my paw at mathematics, please," he announced amid applause from the audience.

"Crikey!" exclaimed Jonathan. "Fancy choosing maths!"

"Knowing the way Paddington does the shopping," said Mrs Bird, "I think it's a very wise choice."

Paddington had a reputation among the street traders in the Portobello market for striking a hard bargain and it was generally acknowledged that you had to get up very early in the morning indeed in order to get the better of him.

"I must say he always keeps his accounts very neatly," said Mrs Brown. "I'm sure it's the right choice."

"Mathematics?" repeated Ronnie Playfair. "Well, we'd better look for the first question." He put his hand into one of the barrels and withdrew a piece of paper. "A nice easy one to start with," he announced approvingly, "and a very good question for a bear. If you get it right there's a prize of five pounds."

After a short roll of drums Ronnie Playfair raised his hand for silence. "For a prize of five pounds," he announced. "How many buns make five?"

"I must warn you," he added, winking at the audience, "think carefully. It may be a trick question. How many buns make five?"

Paddington thought for a moment. "Two and a half," he replied.

Ronnie Playfair's jaw dropped slightly. "Two and a half?" he repeated. "Are you sure you won't change your mind?"

"Two and a half," said Paddington firmly.

"Poor old Paddington," said Jonathan. "Fancy getting the first one wrong."

"I am surprised," said Mrs Bird. "It's not like him at all. Unless he's got something up his paw."

"Oh dear," said the Master of Ceremonies as he picked up a hammer and struck a large gong by his side. "I'm afraid you're out of the contest. The answer is five."

"I don't think it is, Mr Playfair," said Paddington. "It's two and a half. I always share my buns with Mr Gruber when we have our elevenses and I break them in half."

Ronnie Playfair's jaw dropped even farther and the smile froze on his face. "You share your buns with Mr Gruber?" he repeated.

"Give him the money!" cried someone in the audience as the applause died down.

"You said it might be a trick question," cried someone else amid laughter. "Now you've got a trick answer."

Ronnie Playfair fingered his collar nervously and a strange look came over his face as he received a signal from the man wearing headphones to give Paddington the money.

"Are you going to stop now, bear?" he asked hopefully, as he handed Paddington a crisp five-pound note, "or do you want to go on for the next prize of fifty pounds?"

"I'd like to go on please, Mr Playfair," said Paddington eagerly, as he hurriedly locked the money away in his suitcase.

"I shouldn't do that," said Ronnie Playfair as he dipped his hand into the barrel and withdrew another piece of paper. "If you get this question wrong I shall want the five pounds back."

"Oh dear," said Mrs Brown. "I feel all turned over inside. I hope Paddington doesn't do anything silly and lose his five pounds. He'll be so upset we shall never hear the last of it."

"Right!" said Ronnie Playfair, holding up his hand once again for silence. "For fifty pounds here is question number two, and it's a two-part question. Listen carefully."

"If," he said, "you had a piece of wood eight feet long and you cut it in half, and if you cut the two pieces you then have into half, and if you then cut all the pieces into half again how many pieces would you have?"

"Eight," said Paddington promptly.

"Very good, bear," said Ronnie Playfair

approvingly. "Now," he continued, pointing to a large clock by his side, "here is the second part of the question. How long will each of the pieces be? You have ten seconds to answer starting from… now!"

"Eight feet," said Paddington, almost before the Master of Ceremonies had time to start the clock.

"Eight feet?" repeated Ronnie Playfair. "You're sure you won't change your mind?"

"No, thank you, Mr Playfair," said Paddington firmly.

"In that case," said Ronnie Playfair as he triumphantly banged the gong, "I must ask for the five pounds back. The answer is one foot. If I had a piece of wood eight feet long and I cut it in half I would have two pieces four feet long. And if I cut those in half I would have four pieces two feet long. And if I cut each of those in half I would have eight pieces one foot long."

Having finished his speech Ronnie Playfair turned and beamed a self-satisfied smile on the audience. "You can't argue with that, bear," he exclaimed.

"Oh no, Mr Playfair," said Paddington politely. "I'm sure that's right for *your* piece of wood, but I cut mine the other way."

Once again the smile froze on Ronnie Playfair's face. "You did *what*?" he exclaimed.

"I cut mine down the middle," said Paddington. "So I had eight pieces eight feet long."

"But if you're asked to cut a plank of wood in half," stuttered Ronnie Playfair, "you cut it across the middle not *down* the middle. It stands to reason."

"Not if you're a bear," said Paddington, remembering his efforts at carpentry in the past. "If you're a bear it's safer to cut it down the middle."

Ronnie Playfair took a deep breath and forced a sickly smile to his face as he handed Paddington a large bundle of notes.

"I think you'll find they're all there, bear," he said stiffly as Paddington sat down on the stage and began counting them. "We're not in the habit of diddling people."

Ronnie Playfair looked anxiously at his watch. The programme seemed to be taking a lot longer than usual. Normally he would have got through at least five contestants by now.

"There are only five minutes left," he said. "Do you want to go for the final prize of five hundred pounds?"

"Five hundred pounds!" exclaimed Judy in a tone of awe.

"If I were Paddington," said Mrs Brown, "I'd stop now and make sure of what I've got."

The Browns grouped themselves even closer round their television screen as one of the cameras showed a close-up picture of Paddington considering the matter.

"I think I would like to carry on, Mr Playfair," he announced at last amid a burst of applause.

Although Paddington was not the sort of bear who normally believed in taking too many chances as far as money was concerned he was much too excited by all that had taken place that evening to think clearly about the matter.

"Well," said Ronnie Playfair in his most solemn voice, "Here, for a prize of five hundred pounds is the last question of the evening, and this time it's a much harder one."

"It would be," said Mrs Brown, holding her breath.

"If," continued Ronnie Playfair, "it takes two men twenty minutes to fill a fifty-gallon bath full of water using one tap, how long will it take one man to fill the same bath using both taps. This time you've got twenty seconds starting from… now!"

Ronnie Playfair pressed a button on the clock by his side and then stood back to await Paddington's answer.

"No time at all, Mr Playfair," said Paddington promptly.

"Wrong!" exclaimed Ronnie Playfair, as a groan came up from the audience. "I'm afraid this time you really have got it wrong. It will take exactly half the time.

"I'm very sorry, bear," he continued, looking most relieved as he gave the gong a bang with his hammer. "Better luck next time."

"I think you must be wrong, Mr Playfair," said Paddington politely.

"Nonsense," said the Master of Ceremonies, giving Paddington a nasty look. "The answer's on the card. In any case it's bound to take some time. You can't fill a bath in no time at all."

"But you said it was the same bath," explained Paddington. "The first two men had already filled it once, and you didn't say anything about pulling the plug out."

Ronnie Playfair's face seemed to go a strange purple colour in the studio, and even on the Browns' receiver it went several shades darker as he stared at Paddington. "I didn't say anything about them pulling the plug out?" he repeated. "But of course they pulled it out."

"You didn't say so," cried a voice in the audience as several boos broke out. "That bear's quite right."

"Give him the money!" cried someone else as several more voices added to the general uproar.

Ronnie Playfair seemed to shudder slightly as he withdrew a silk handkerchief from his jacket pocket and patted his brow. "Congratulations, bear," he said grudgingly, after a long pause. "You've won the jackpot!"

"What!" exclaimed Paddington hotly, as he gave Ronnie Playfair one of his hardest ever stares. "I've won a *jackpot*? I thought you said it was five hundred pounds."

"That *is* five hundred pounds," said Ronnie Playfair hastily. "It's the top prize of all. That's why it's called a jackpot."

As the applause rang through the theatre Paddington sat down on his suitcase hardly able to believe his ears. Although he knew there must be five hundred pounds in the world he had never in his wildest dreams thought he might one day see it in one big pile, let alone be told it was his.

Ronnie Playfair held up his hand for silence. "One final question before we end the programme," he exclaimed. "And there's no prize for this one. What are you going to do with all the money?"

Paddington considered the matter for a long time as the audience went very quiet. When you usually counted your money in terms of how many buns it would buy it was very difficult to even begin to think about a sum like five hundred pounds let alone decide what to do with it, and when he tried to think of five hundred pounds worth of buns he grew quite dizzy.

"I think," he said at last, as the camera came closer and closer, "I would like to keep a little bit as a souvenir and to buy some Christmas presents. Then I would like to give the rest to the Home for Retired Bears in Lima."

"The Home for Retired Bears in Lima?" repeated Ronnie Playfair, looking most surprised.

"That's right," said Paddington. "That's where my Aunt Lucy lives. She's very happy there but I don't think they've got very much money. They only have marmalade on Sundays so I expect they would find it very useful."

Everyone applauded Paddington's announcement and the applause grew louder still a few moment later when Ronnie Playfair announced on behalf of the television company that they would see to it the Home for Retired Bears in Lima was well supplied with marmalade for at least a year to come.

"After all," he said, "it isn't every week a bear wins the jackpot in one of our quiz programmes."

"Well I'm blowed," said Mr Brown, mopping his brow as the programme came to an end and the captions began rolling past on the screen over a picture of Paddington as he stood in the middle of the stage receiving everyone's congratulations. "I never thought when we bought a television set it would come to this."

"Fancy Paddington giving it away," said Jonathan. "He's usually so careful with his money."

"Careful isn't the same as being mean," said Mrs Bird wisely. "And I must say I'm very glad. I never did like the thought of all those bears only having marmalade on Sundays."

"After all," she added amid general agreement, "if it hadn't been for Aunt Lucy we shouldn't have met Paddington. And if that doesn't deserve a bit of extra marmalade I don't know what does."

Chapter Five

A STICKY TIME

Mrs Bird paused for a moment and sniffed the air as she and Mrs Brown turned the corner into Windsor Gardens. "Can you smell something?" she asked.

Mrs Brown stopped by her side. Now that Mrs Bird mentioned it there *was* a very peculiar odour coming from somewhere near at hand. It wasn't exactly unpleasant but it was rather sweet and sickly and it seemed to be made up of a number of things she couldn't quite place.

"Perhaps there's been a bonfire somewhere," she remarked as they picked up their shopping and continued along the road.

"Whatever it is," said Mrs Bird darkly, "it seems to be getting worse. In fact," she added, as they neared number thirty-two, "it's much too close to home for my liking."

"I knew it!" she exclaimed, as they made their way along the drive at the side of the house. "Just look at my kitchen windows!"

"Oh dear," said Mrs Brown as she followed the direction of Mrs Bird's gaze. "What on earth has that bear been up to now?"

Looking at Mrs Bird's kitchen windows it seemed just as if, in some strange way, someone had changed them for frosted glass while they had been out. Worse still, not only did the glass have a frosted appearance, but there were several tiny rivers of a rather nasty-looking brown liquid trickling down them as well, and from a small, partly open window at the top there came a steady cloud of escaping steam.

While Mrs Bird examined the outside of her kitchen windows Mrs Brown hurried round to the back of the house. "I do hope Paddington's all right," she exclaimed when she returned. "I can't get in through the back door. It seems to be stuck."

"Hmm," said Mrs Bird grimly. "If the windows look like this from the outside heaven alone knows what we shall find when we get indoors."

Normally the windows at number thirty-two Windsor Gardens were kept spotlessly clean, with never a trace of a smear, but even Mrs Bird began to look worried as she peered in vain for a gap in the mist through which she could see what was going on.

Had she but known, the chances of seeing anything at all through the haze were more unlikely than she imagined, for on the other side of the glass even Paddington was having to admit to himself that things were getting a bit out of hand.

In fact, as he groped his way across the kitchen in the direction of the stove, where

several large saucepans stood bubbling and giving forth clouds of steam, he decided he didn't much like the look of the few things he could see.

Climbing up on a kitchen chair he lifted the lid off one of the saucepans and peered hopefully inside as he poked at the contents with one of Mrs Bird's tablespoons. The mixture was much stiffer than he had expected and it was as much as he could manage to push the spoon in let alone stir with it.

Paddington's whiskers began to droop in the steam as he worked the spoon back and forth, but it wasn't until he tried to take it out in order to test the result of his labours that a really worried expression came over his face, for to his surprise however much he pulled and tugged it wouldn't even budge.

The more he struggled the hotter the spoon became and after a moment or two he gave it up as a bad job and hurriedly let go of the handle as he climbed back down off the chair in order to consult a large magazine which was lying open on the floor.

Making toffee wasn't at all the easy thing the article in the magazine made it out to be and it was all most disappointing, particularly as it was the first time he'd tried his paw at making sweets.

The magazine in question was an old one of Mrs Brown's and he had first come across it earlier in the day when he'd been at a bit of a loose end. Normally Paddington didn't think much of Mrs Brown's magazines. They were much too full of advertisements and items about how to keep clean and look smart for his liking, but this one had caught his eye because it was a special cookery number.

On the cover there was a picture showing a golden brown roast chicken resting on a plate laden with bright green peas, bread sauce, and roast potatoes. Alongside the chicken there was a huge sundae oozing with layer upon layer of fruit and ice-cream, while beyond that was a large wooden board laden with so many different kinds of cheese that Paddington had soon lost count of the number as he lay on his bed licking his whiskers.

The inside of the magazine had been even more interesting and it had taken him some while to get through the coloured photographs alone.

But it was the last article of all which had really made him sit up and take notice. It was called TEN EASY WAYS WITH TOFFEE, and it was written by a lady called Granny Green who lived in the country and seemed to spend all her time making sweets.

Granny Green appeared in quite a number of the pictures and whenever she did it was always alongside a pile of freshly made Old Fashioned Humbugs, a dish of coconut ice or a mound of some other sweet-meat.

Paddington had read the article several times with a great deal of interest for although in the past he'd tried his paw at cooking various kinds of dinner he'd never before heard of anyone making sweets at home and it seemed a very good idea indeed.

All Granny Green's recipes looked nice but it was the last one of all, for Olde Fashioned Butter Toffee, that had really made Paddington's mouth water. Even Granny Green herself seemed to like it best for in one picture she was actually caught helping herself to a piece behind her kitchen door when she thought no one was watching.

It not only looked very tempting but Paddington decided it was very good value for money as well, for apart from using condensed milk and sugar, all that was needed was butter, treacle, and some stuff called vanilla essence, all of which Mrs Bird kept in her store cupboard.

After checking carefully through the recipe once more Paddington took another look at the magazine in the hope of seeing where he'd gone wrong but none of the photographs were any help at all. All Granny Green's saucepans were as bright as a new pin with not a trace of anything sticky running down the sides, and even her spoons were laid out neat and shining on the kitchen table. There was certainly no mention of any of them getting stuck in the toffee.

In any case her toffee was a light golden brown colour and it was cut into neat squares and laid out on a plate, whereas, from what he'd been able to make out of his own through the steam, it was more the colour of dark brown boot polish, and even if he had been able to get it out of the saucepans he couldn't for the life of him think what he could cut it with.

Paddington rather wished he'd tried one of the other nine recipes instead and after heaving a deep sigh he groped his way across the kitchen and stretching up a paw rubbed a hole in the steam on one of the window panes. As he did so he jumped back into the

middle of the room with a gasp of alarm, for there, on the other side of the glass, was the familiar face of Mrs Bird.

Mrs Bird appeared to be saying something and although he couldn't make out the actual words he didn't like the look of some of them at all. Fortunately, before she was able to say very much the glass clouded over again and Paddington sat down in the middle of the kitchen floor with a forlorn expression on his face as he awaited developments.

He hadn't long to wait for a few moments later there came the sound of footsteps in the hall. "What on earth's been going on?" cried Mrs Bird, as she burst through the door.

"I've been trying my paw at toffee making, Mrs Bird," explained Paddington sadly.

"Toffee making!" exclaimed Mrs Brown, as she flung open the window. "Why, you could cut the air with a knife."

"That's more than you can say for the toffee," said Mrs Bird, as she pulled at the end of the spoon Paddington had left in the saucepan. "It looks more like glue."

"I'm afraid it is a bit thick, Mrs Bird," said Paddington. "I think I must have got my Granny Greens mixed up by mistake."

"I don't know about your Granny Greens," said Mrs Bird grimly, as she surveyed the scene. "It looks as if you've got the whole pantry mixed up. I only cleaned the kitchen this morning and now look at it!"

Paddington half stood up and gazed around the room. Now that most of the steam had cleared it looked in rather more of a mess than he had expected. There were several large pools of treacle on the floor and a long trail of sugar leading from the table to the stove, not to mention two or three half-open tins of condensed milk lying on their side where they had fallen off the draining board.

"It's a job to know where to start," said Mrs Brown, as she stepped gingerly over one of the treacle pools. "I've never seen such a mess."

"Well, we shan't get it cleared up if we stand looking at it, that's a certainty," said Mrs Bird briskly as she bustled around sweeping everything in sight into the sink. "I suggest a certain young bear had better get down on his paws and knees with a scrubbing brush and a bowl of water before he's very much older, otherwise we shall all get stuck to the floor."

Mrs Bird paused. While she'd been talking a strange expression had come over Paddington's face, one which she didn't like the look of at all. "Is anything the matter?" she asked.

"I'm not sure, Mrs Bird," said Paddington, as he made several attempts to stand up and then hurriedly sat down again holding his stomach with both paws. "I've got a bit of a pain."

"You haven't been *eating* this stuff have you?" exclaimed Mrs Brown, pointing to the saucepans.

"Well, I did test it once or twice, Mrs Brown," said Paddington.

"Gracious me!" cried Mrs Bird. "No wonder you've got a pain. It's probably set in a hard lump in your inside."

"Try standing up again," said Mrs Brown anxiously.

"I don't think I can," gasped Paddington, as he lay back on the floor. "I think it's getting worse."

"That poor bear," cried Mrs Bird, all thoughts of the mess in the kitchen banished from her mind as she hurried into the hall. "We must ring for Doctor MacAndrew at once."

Mrs Bird was only gone a moment or so before the door burst open again. "The doctor's out on his rounds," she said. "They don't know when he'll be back and they can't even find his locum."

"They can't find his locum!" repeated Paddington, looking more worried than ever.

"That's his assistant," explained Mrs Brown. "There's nothing to get upset about."

"We could try a strong dose of castor oil, I suppose," she continued, turning to Mrs Bird.

"I've a feeling it'll need more than castor oil," said Mrs Bird ominously, as Paddington jumped up hurriedly with a 'feeling better' expression on his face and then gave a loud groan as he promptly sat down again. "I've sent for the ambulance."

"The ambulance!" cried Mrs Brown, going quite pale. "Oh dear."

"We should never forgive ourselves," said Mrs Bird wisely, "if anything happened to that bear."

So saying she put her arms underneath Paddington and lifting him gently, carried him into the dining-room and placed him on the sofa where he lay with his legs sticking up in the air.

Leaving Paddington where he was, Mrs Bird disappeared upstairs and when she returned she was carrying a small leather suitcase. "I've packed all his washing things," she explained to Mrs Brown. "And I've put in a jar of his special marmalade in case he needs it."

Mrs Bird mentioned the last item in a loud voice in the hope that it would cheer Paddington up but at the mention of the word marmalade a loud groan came from the direction of the sofa.

Mrs Brown and Mrs Bird exchanged glances. If the thought of marmalade made Paddington feel worse then things must be very bad indeed.

"I'd better ring Henry at the office," said Mrs Brown as she hurried out into the hall. "I'll get him to come home straight away."

Fortunately, as Mrs Brown replaced the telephone receiver, and before they had time to worry about the matter any more, there came the sound of a loud bell ringing outside followed by a squeal of brakes and a bang on the front door.

"Ho dear," said the ambulance man as he entered the dining-room and saw Paddington lying on the sofa. "What's this? I was told it was an emergency. Nobody said anything about it being a bear."

"Bears have emergencies the same as anyone else," said Mrs Bird sternly. "Now just you bring your stretcher and hurry up about it."

The ambulance man scratched his head. "I don't know what they're going to say back at the hospital," he said doubtfully. "They've got an 'out-patients' and an 'in-patients' department, but I've never come across a 'bear-patients' department before."

"Well, they're going to have one now," said Mrs Bird. "And if that bear isn't in it by the time five minutes is up I shall want to know the reason why."

The ambulance man looked nervously at Mrs Bird and then back at the sofa as Paddington gave another loud groan. "I must say he doesn't look too good," he remarked.

"He's all right when he's got his legs in

the air," explained Mrs Brown. "It's when he tries to put them down it hurts."

The ambulance man came to a decision. The combination of Mrs Bird's glares and Paddington's groans was too much for him. "Bert," he called through the open door. "Fetch the number one stretcher. And look slippy. We've a young bear emergency in here and I don't much like the look of him."

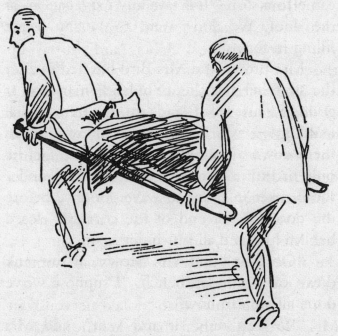

Nobody spoke in the ambulance on the way to the hospital. Mrs Bird, Mrs Brown, and the man in charge travelled in the back with Paddington, and all the while his legs got higher and higher until by the time the ambulance turned in through the hospital gates they were almost doubled back on themselves.

Even the ambulance man looked worried. "Never seen anything like it before," he said.

"I'll cover him over with a blanket, Ma'am," he continued to Mrs Bird as they came to a stop. "It'll save any explanations at the door. We don't want too many delays filling in forms."

Mrs Brown and Mrs Bird hurried in after the stretcher but the ambulance man was as good as his word and in no time at all Paddington was being whisked away from them down a long white corridor. In fact he only had time to poke a paw out from under the blanket in order to wave goodbye before the doors at the end of the corridor closed behind him and all was quiet again.

"Oh dear," said Mrs Brown, as she sank down on a wooden bench. "I suppose we've done all we can now."

"We can only sit and wait," said Mrs Bird gravely as she sat down beside her. "Wait and hope."

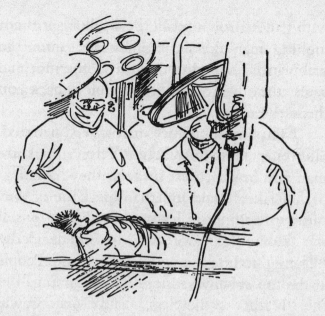

The Browns and Mr Gruber sat in a miserable group in the corridor as they watched the comings and goings of the nurses. Mr Brown had arrived soon after the ambulance, bringing with him Jonathan and Judy, and shortly after that Mr Gruber had turned up carrying a bunch of flowers and a huge bag of grapes.

"They're from the traders in the market," he explained. "They all send their best wishes and hope he soon gets well."

"It won't be long now," said Mr Brown as several nurses entered the room at the end of the corridor. "I think things are beginning to happen."

As Mr Brown spoke a tall, distinguished-looking man dressed from head to foot in green came hurrying down the corridor and with a nod in their direction disappeared through the same door.

"That must be Sir Mortimer Carroway," said Judy knowledgeably. "That ambulance man said he's the best surgeon they have."

"Crikey!" said Jonathan in a tone of awe. "Fancy Paddington having him!"

"Quite right too," said Mrs Bird decidedly. "There's nothing like going to the top. People at the top are always more understanding."

"I feel so helpless," said Mrs Brown, voicing the thoughts of them all as they sat on the bench and prepared themselves for a long wait. They were each of them busy with their own thoughts and although not one of them would have admitted it to the others, even the knowledge that such a famous person as Sir Mortimer Carroway was in charge didn't help matters.

"Good heavens!" exclaimed Mr Brown a few minutes later as the door at the end of the corridor opened once again and the figure of Sir Mortimer appeared. "That was quick."

Mrs Brown clutched her husband's arm. "You don't think anything's gone wrong do you, Henry?" she asked.

"We shall soon know," said Mr Brown, as Sir Mortimer caught sight of them and came hurrying along the corridor holding a piece of fur in his hand.

"Are you that young bear's... er... next of kin?" he asked.

"Well, he lives with us," said Mrs Brown.

"He *is* going to be all right?" exclaimed Judy, looking anxiously at the piece of fur.

"I should think," said Sir Mortimer in a grave voice, but with the suspicion of a twinkle in his eyes, "there's every chance he'll pull through."

"Gracious me!" exclaimed Mrs Bird as there was a sudden commotion at the end of the corridor. "There *is* Paddington. Don't tell me he's up already."

"A bad case of galloping toffee drips," said Sir Mortimer. "Most unusual. On the stomach too. Worst possible place."

"Galloping toffee drips?" repeated Mr Brown.

"I think I must have spilt some on my fur when I was testing it, Mr Brown," explained Paddington as he joined them.

"They probably set when he was sitting down," said Sir Mortimer. "No wonder he couldn't get up again."

Sir Mortimer chuckled at the look on everyone's face. "I'm afraid he'll have a bare patch for a week or so but I don't doubt if you keep him on a diet of marmalade for a while it'll start to grow again. It should be all right by Christmas."

"If you don't mind, bear," he said as he made to leave, "I'd like to keep this piece of fur as a souvenir. I've done a good few operations in my time but I've never had a bear's emergency before."

"What a good job Sir Mortimer had a sense of humour," said Mrs Brown as they all drove home in Mr Brown's car. "I can't imagine what some surgeons would have said."

"Fancy keeping Paddington's fur as a

souvenir," said Judy. "I wonder if he'll have it framed."

Looking out from behind Mr Gruber's bunch of grapes Paddington gave the rest of the carload one of his injured expressions. He felt very upset that everyone was taking his operation so lightly now that it had turned out all right, especially as he had a cold spot in the middle of his stomach where Sir Mortimer had removed the fur.

"Perhaps," said Mr Gruber, as they turned into Windsor Gardens, "he just likes bears.

"After all, Mr Brown," he added, turning to Paddington, "joking aside, it might have been serious and it's nice to know there *are* people like that in the world you can turn to in times of trouble."

And to that remark even Paddington had to nod his wholehearted agreement.

Chapter Six

TROUBLE IN THE
BARGAIN BASEMENT

Soon after the toffee-making episode a
change came over the weather. The air
suddenly became crisper and often in the
mornings a thin film of ice covered the
windows with a pattern of tiny ferns so that
Paddington had to breathe quite heavily on
his panes before he could see into the garden.
Even when he did manage to make a hole
large enough to see through his effort was
usually only rewarded by the sight of an even
larger expanse of white outside.

Almost overnight great piles of fir trees
arrived in the market and on the barrows
brightly coloured boxes of figs and dates put

in an appearance alongside branches of holly and sprigs of mistletoe.

Inside the house there were changes too, as bowls of fruit and nuts began to appear on the sideboard and mysterious-looking lists were hastily tucked into jugs whenever he came into a room.

"Christmas comes but once a year," said Mrs Bird, when she met Paddington in the hall one morning on his return from the market, "and when it does it's time for certain young bears to have a bath, otherwise they may find themselves left behind when we go on our shopping expedition this afternoon."

As Mrs Bird disappeared into the kitchen Paddington stared with wide-open eyes at the closed door for a moment or two and then hurried upstairs as fast as his legs would carry him.

The year before, Mrs Brown and Mrs Bird had taken him to a big London store in order to do the Christmas shopping, and although for some weeks past he had been keeping his paws firmly crossed in the hope that they would take him again, the news still came as a great surprise.

Paddington spent the rest of the morning hurrying round busily making his preparations for the big event. Apart from having a bath, there was so much to do in the way of making out lists and sorting through the various things he wanted to take with him, not to mention finding space for a hurried lunch, that it seemed no time at all before he found himself being helped off a bus as it stopped outside a large and familiar-looking building in one of the big London streets.

"I thought we would try and do most of our shopping at Barkridges," explained Mrs Brown, when she saw Paddington's look of surprise. "It's so much easier if you can get everything in the one shop."

Paddington peered up at the building with renewed interest for he hadn't visited Barkridge's store since his very first shopping expedition and it looked quite different now all the Christmas decorations were up. Apart from gaily coloured displays in all the windows the outside of the building was a mass of fairy lights which hung from some of the biggest Christmas trees he had ever seen in his life and altogether it looked most inviting.

"I think I'd like to do some shopping by myself, Mrs Brown," he exclaimed eagerly. "I've got one or two special things to buy."

Mrs Brown and Mrs Bird exchanged glances. "I suppose we could let him go down to the bargain basement," said Mrs Bird as they entered the shop. "If we wait at the top of the stairs he can't come to any great harm."

Paddington pricked up his ears at Mrs Bird's words. He had never been down to a bargain basement before and it sounded most interesting.

Mrs Brown looked at him doubtfully. "Well," she said, "it is Christmas. But you must promise to be back here in half an hour. We've a lot to do."

"Thank you very much, Mrs Brown," said Paddington gratefully as he picked up his belongings and hurried off in the direction of some nearby stairs.

"Hmm," said Mrs Bird, voicing both their thoughts as Paddington disappeared through a door at the bottom. "That bear was in too much of a hurry for my liking. I've a nasty feeling in the back of my mind we're letting ourselves in for trouble."

"Even Paddington can't come to much harm in half an hour," said Mrs Brown optimistically. "Not with shopping to do."

"If he gets as far as the shopping," said Mrs Bird darkly.

Unaware of the way he was being discussed, Paddington stood for a moment blinking happily in the bright lights of the bargain basement. If anything, it was even more crowded than the upstairs had been and there was so much to see it was difficult to take it all in at one glance.

In front of him there was a big signpost with arrows pointing the way to the various departments and after studying it for a moment or two he decided to investigate the one marked KITCHEN AND HOUSEHOLD. Apart from the fact that he felt sure the Household department of a big store like Barkridges would be bound to have something suitable for Mrs Bird's present, he had just caught sight of another interesting notice pasted on the wall. It said THIS WAY TO THE FREE DEMONSTRATIONS, and it definitely needed looking into.

Following the arrows, Paddington made his way along a corridor until he found himself standing in a large area full of pots and pans. All around people were shouting and jostling and as he put his head down and pushed his way through he suddenly discovered to his surprise that he had come up against a large table behind which stood a

man in a white coat. The man appeared to be doing something with a piece of old carpet and a bottle and he didn't look best pleased at the way things were going.

"Look at that!" he shouted, holding up the piece of carpet as Paddington stood on tip-toe in order to get a better view. "Only one coating of Instant One-dab cleaning fluid and already this old piece of carpet looks like new!"

"Come on, ladies," he cried in a hoarse voice. "There must be someone who wants to buy a bottle. It not only cleans carpets – just one dab on your kitchen sink and you'll be able to see your face in it. Mirrors, furniture, floors – there's nothing in the world that can't be improved by Instant One-dab cleaning fluid. I'm not asking fifteen pence for it. I'm not even asking ten pence. All I want for this giant-size economy bottle is the trifling sum of seven pence."

Pausing for breath the man looked at the sea of faces in front of him. "Some people can't see a bargain when it's held in front of their nose," he said crossly as no one moved.

"Take this piece of stuff here," he continued, as he reached out across the table and picked up a shapeless-looking object which he held up for everyone to see. "You couldn't have anything much dirtier than this. Most of you would probably have thrown it away years ago. Yet I guarantee that with one dab of my cleaning fluid it'll come up as good as new."

"What!" cried Paddington in alarm, as he clambered up on his suitcase. "That's my hat you've got!"

"Your hat?" exclaimed the man, dropping it hurriedly. "I beg your pardon, sir. I didn't realize anyone was *wearing* it. I thought it was one of my old scraps I get off the dustman. I keep a few of them by me for demonstrations you know…"

The man's voice trailed away as he caught

Paddington's eye. "I was only trying to get rid of your stains," he said lamely.

"Get rid of my stains?" repeated Paddington, hardly able to believe his ears. It had taken him a long time to collect all the different stains on his hat. Some of them were so old he had almost forgotten how they had got there in the first place, and some had even been made by his uncle in Peru.

"Those aren't ordinary stains," he exclaimed hotly. "Some of them have been handed down."

"Handed down?" echoed the man. "You can't hand a stain down."

"Bears do," said Paddington firmly.

The demonstration man gave a nasty look. "Well, if you want to hand them down any more," he said, waving the bottle of cleaning fluid dangerously close to Paddington's hat, "I suggest you hop it. This is very powerful stuff and if the cork comes out accidentally I shan't answer for the consequences."

Grabbing his hat Paddington pulled it tightly down over his head and pushed his way through the crowd out of range of the man's bottle. He didn't think much of the first demonstration he'd seen, even if it had been free, and he hurriedly made his way in the direction of the second one in the hope that it might prove more interesting.

As he approached the next crowd Paddington paused for a moment and sniffed the air. To his surprise there seemed to be a strong smell of pancakes and as he squeezed his way towards the demonstration it got stronger and stronger until by the time he reached the table he felt quite hungry.

This time the man in charge had a small spirit stove in front of him and he was holding a frying-pan in the air while he addressed his audience.

"How many times," he cried, as Paddington reached the table. "How many times have you broken your fried eggs in the morning? How many omelets have you spoilt at lunch-time? And have you ever kept count of the number of times you've tried tossing a pancake only to find it stuck to the pan?"

Holding up the frying-pan for everyone to see, the demonstration man paused dramatically. "Never again!" he cried, as he waved it in the air. "Go home today and throw your old pans in the dustbin. Buy one of my Magic Non-stick frying-pans and nothing, I repeat, *nothing* will ever stick again."

"Why, it's so simple," he went on, "even a child of five can't go wrong.

"Come along sir," he exclaimed, pointing to Paddington. "Show everyone how to do it."

"Stand back everyone," he called, as he handed the frying-pan to Paddington. "The young gentleman with the whiskers is going to show you all how easy it is to toss a pancake with one of my Magic Non-stick frying-pans."

"Thank you very much," said Paddington gratefully. "I might buy one for Mrs Bird's Christmas present," he explained. "She's always grumbling about her pans."

"There you are," said the demonstration man triumphantly. "My first sale of the morning. Fancy all of you being put to shame by a young bear gentleman."

"I can see you know your frying-pans as well as your onions, sir," he continued, as Paddington gripped the frying-pan firmly in both paws and closed his eyes as he prepared to test it. "Now, just a quick flick of the paw, and don't forget to catch the pancake on the way down otherwise…"

Whatever else the man had been about to say was lost as a gasp went up from the audience. "Here," he cried anxiously, "what have you done with it?"

"What have I done with it?" said Paddington with interest as he opened his eyes and peered at the empty pan.

"That was my demonstration pancake," cried the man, looking all around. "And now it's gone!"

The problem of where the pancake had disappeared to was suddenly solved as a disturbance broke out at the back of the crowd and a woman started to push her way through to the front.

"My best hat!" she exclaimed. "Covered in pancake mixture!"

"Never mind your hat," cried someone else. "What about my coat?"

As more and more voices joined in the uproar Paddington decided to take advantage of the confusion. Picking up his suitcase and carrier bag he hurried out of the Household department casting some extremely anxious glances over his shoulder as he went. He didn't like the look of things at all and he decided he'd had quite enough of free demonstrations for one day.

It was as he was hurrying in the direction of the stairs and safety that Paddington suddenly stopped in his tracks again and peered up at the wall. In front of him was a large poster which he hadn't noticed before showing a man in a white beard and a long red coat sitting astride a rocket. But it wasn't so much the picture which caught his eye as the wording underneath.

It said:

TRIPS TO THE MOON
VISIT FATHER CHRISTMAS IN THE MOON ROCKET
GET YOUR FREE PRESENT
TEN PENCE RETURN!

After the wording a broad red arrow decorated with holly pointed the way towards a door in front of which stood a group of people.

Paddington considered the matter for a moment. Ten pence seemed very cheap for a trip to the moon, especially as it had cost Mrs Brown almost as much for the three of them on the bus and they hadn't even been given a present at the end.

Although he'd promised Mrs Brown and Mrs Bird to stay in the bargain basement Paddington felt sure they wouldn't mind in the circumstances if he took a short trip. At that moment the doors opened and the matter was decided for him as he was caught up in the rush of people all pushing and shoving to get through. In fact it all happened so quickly he only just found time to hand his ten pence piece to the man in uniform before the doors clanged shut behind him.

"Thank you very much," called the man, touching his cap as Paddington was swept past him. "A Merry Christmas to you."

Paddington tried to raise his hat in reply but by that time he was so tightly jammed against the wall at the back that he hardly had room to breathe let alone move his paws. In fact he was so squashed that it only took him a moment or two to decide very firmly indeed that he didn't think much of rockets.

Apart from the fact that it kept stopping, it was so crowded he couldn't see a thing. And when it did finally reach the top of its travel even more people pushed their way in before he had a chance to clamber out and it started to fall back down again without his having so much as caught a glimpse of Father Christmas.

Altogether Paddington wasn't sorry when he heard the man in charge announce the fact that they were back in the bargain basement again and it was time to get out.

"I'd like my present now, please," he exclaimed, as he pushed his way out behind the other passengers.

"Your *present*?" said the man in uniform. "What present?"

Paddington gave the man a hard stare. "The one the notice says you get," he explained.

The man looked puzzled for a moment and then his face cleared as Paddington pointed to the poster. "You want Father Christmas on the fourth floor," he said. "We don't give presents here. This is the lift, not a rocket."

"What!" cried Paddington, nearly falling over backwards with surprise. "This is a lift? But I gave you ten pence."

"That's right, sir," said the man cheerfully. "Thank you very much. It isn't often we liftmen get a Christmas box."

"A Christmas box?" echoed Paddington, his eyes getting larger and larger.

"Very kind of you it was," said the liftman. "And now if you'll excuse me I've another load to take up."

With that he clanged the doors shut leaving Paddington fixed to the spot as if he had been turned into a pillar of stone. He was still rooted to the spot several minutes later when Mrs Brown and Mrs Bird came hurrying up accompanied by an important-looking man in striped trousers.

"Where on earth have you been?" cried Mrs Bird. "We've been looking everywhere for you."

"Are you all right?" asked Mrs Brown anxiously. "You don't look very well."

"Oh, I'm all right, thank you, Mrs Brown," said Paddington vaguely as he recovered himself. "And I haven't been on earth — at least, I have, but I didn't think I had and it cost me ten pence."

The rest of Paddington's explanations were lost as the man in the striped trousers bounded forward and shook him warmly by

the paw. "My dear young bear," he exclaimed, "I'm the floor manager. Allow me to thank you for all you've done."

"That's all right," said Paddington, looking most surprised as he raised his hat.

"Non-stick frying pans have never been one of our most popular lines," said the floor manager as he turned to Mrs Brown. "And as for the cleaning fluid... now look at them both." He waved his hand in the direction of two large crowds in the distance. "They're both selling like hot cakes.

"Since this young bear demonstrated the frying-pan our man can't wrap them fast enough. And after our other assistant removed the pancake stains from the customers' clothes he's been rushed off his feet. Anything that gets a young bear's pancake stain out without leaving a mark must be good.

"You must let me know if there's anything we can do to repay you," he continued, turning back to Paddington.

Paddington thought for a moment. "I was doing some special Christmas shopping," he explained. "Only I'm not really sure what I want to buy. It's a bit difficult for bears to see over the edge of the counters."

"In that case," said the floor manager, snapping his fingers in the direction of one of the assistants, "you shall have the services of one of our expert shopping advisers. She can look after you for the rest of the day and I'm sure she'll be only too pleased to help you with all your needs."

"Thank you very much," said Paddington gratefully. He wasn't at all sure what it was all about but whatever the reason he felt certain that with the help of anyone as important-sounding as a shopping adviser he ought to be able to get some very good Christmas presents indeed.

As she bent down to pick up her

shopping Mrs Brown caught Mrs Bird's eye. "I wish someone would tell me how Paddington gets away with it," she said.

"You'd have to be a bear yourself to answer that one," said Mrs Bird wisely. "And if you were the question wouldn't arise anyway. Bears have much more important things to think about."

Chapter Seven

PADDINGTON AND THE
CHRISTMAS PANTOMIME

"Harold Price?" said Mrs Brown. "Wants to see me? But I don't know anyone called Harold Price, do I?"

"It's the young man from the big grocery store in the market," said Mrs Bird. "He said it had something to do with their amateur dramatic society."

"You'd better show him in then," said Mrs Brown. Now that Mrs Bird mentioned it she did vaguely remember Harold Price. He was a rather spotty faced young man who served behind the jam counter. But for the life of her she couldn't imagine what that had to do with amateur dramatics.

"I'm so sorry to trouble you," said Mr Price as Mrs Bird ushered him in to the dining-room. "But I expect you know there's a drama festival taking place in the hall round the corner this week."

"You'd like us to buy some tickets?" asked Mrs Brown, reaching for her handbag.

Mr Price shifted uneasily. "Well... er... no, not exactly," he said. "You see, we've entered a play for the last night – that's tomorrow – and we've been let down at the last moment by the man who was going to do the sound effects. I was told you have a young Mr Brown who's very keen on that sort of thing but I'm afraid I've forgotten his christian name."

"Jonathan?" asked Mrs Brown.

Mr Price shook his head. "No, it wasn't Jonathan," he said. "It was a funny sort of name. He's been on television."

"Not *Paddington*?" said Mrs Bird.

"That's it!" exclaimed Mr Price. "Paddington! I knew it was something unusual.

"I wrote this play myself," he continued eagerly. "It's a sort of mystery pantomime and we're hoping it may win a prize. The sound effects are most important and we must have someone reliable by tomorrow night."

"Have you ever met Paddington?" asked Mrs Bird.

"Well, no," said Mr Price. "But I'm sure he could do them, and if he'll come I can let you all have free seats in the front row."

"That's most kind of you," said Mrs Brown. "I don't know what to say. Paddington does make rather a noise sometimes when he's doing things – but I don't know that you'd exactly call them sound effects."

"Please!" appealed Mr Price. "There just isn't anyone else we can ask."

"Well," said Mrs Brown doubtfully, as she paused at the door. "I'll ask him if you like – but he's upstairs doing his accounts at the moment and I'm not sure that he'll want to be disturbed."

Mr Price looked somewhat taken aback when Mrs Brown returned, closely followed by Paddington. "Oh!" he stammered. "I didn't realize you were a... that is... I... er... I expected someone much older."

"Oh, that's all right, Mr Price," said Paddington cheerfully, as he held out his paw. "I'm nearly four. Bears' years are different."

"Er... quite," said Mr Price. "I'm sure they are." He took hold of Paddington's outstretched paw rather gingerly. Mr Price was a sensitive young man and there were one or two old marmalade stains he didn't like the look of, not to mention a quantity of red ink from the debit side of Paddington's accounts which somehow or other managed to transfer itself to his hand.

"You're sure you hadn't anything else planned?" he asked hopefully.

"Oh no," said Paddington. "Besides, I like theatres and I'm good at learning lines."

"Well, they're not actually lines, Paddington," said Mrs Brown nervously. "They're noises."

"Noises?" exclaimed Paddington, looking most surprised. "I've never heard of a 'noises' play before."

Harold Price looked at him doubtfully. "Perhaps we could use you in some of the crowd scenes," he said. "We're a bit short of serfs."

"Serfs?" exclaimed Paddington.

"That's right," said Mr Price. "All you have to do is come on and say 'Odds bodikins' every now and then."

"Odds bodikins?" repeated Paddington, looking more and more surprised.

"Yes," said Mr Price, growing more enthusiastic at the idea. "And if you do it well

I might even let you say 'Gadzooks' and 'Scurvy knave' as well.'

"Perhaps you'd both like to go into it all down at the hall," said Mrs Brown hastily, as she caught sight of the expression on Paddington's face.

"A very good idea," said Mr Price. "We're just about to start a rehearsal. I can explain it as we go along."

"He did say it's a pantomime?" said Mrs Bird, when she returned from letting Paddington and Mr Price out.

"I think he did," replied Mrs Brown.

"Hmm," said Mrs Bird. "Well, if Paddington has a paw in it there'll be plenty of pantomime – you mark my words!"

"Here we are," said Mr Price, as he showed Paddington through a door marked PRIVATE – ARTISTS ONLY. "I'll take you along and introduce you to the others."

Paddington blinked in the strong lights at the back of the stage and then sniffed. There was a nice smell of greasepaint and it reminded him of the previous time he had been behind the scenes in a theatre, but before he had time to investigate the matter he found himself standing in front of a tall, dark girl who was stretched out on a couch.

"Deirdre," said Mr Price. "I'd like you to meet the young Mr Brown I was telling you about. He's promised to lend a paw with the sound effects."

The dark girl raised herself on one elbow and stared at Paddington. "You didn't tell me he was a *bear*, Harold," she said.

"I didn't know myself… actually," said Mr Price unhappily. "This is Miss Flint, my leading lady," he explained, turning to Paddington. "She's in bacon and eggs."

"How nice," said Paddington, raising his hat politely. "I should like to be in bacon and eggs myself."

"You look rather as if you have been," said Miss Flint, shuddering slightly as she sank back on to the couch. "I suppose the show *must* go on, Harold – but *really*!"

Mr Price looked at Paddington again. "Perhaps you'd better come with me," he said hastily, as he led the way across the stage. "I'll show you what you have to do."

After giving Miss Flint a hard stare Paddington followed Mr Price until they came to a small table in the wings. "This is where you'll be," said Mr Price, picking up a large bundle of papers. "I've marked all the places in the script where there are any sound effects. All you have to do is bang some coconuts together whenever it says 'horses' hooves', and there's a gramophone for when we have any music or thunder noises."

Paddington listened carefully while Mr Price explained about the script and he examined the objects on the table with interest.

"It looks a bit difficult," he said, when Mr Price had finished his explanations, "especially with paws. But I expect it will be all right."

"I hope so," said Mr Price. He ran his hands nervously through his hair and gave Paddington a last worried look as he went back on to the stage to join the rest of the cast. "I do hope so. We've never had a bear doing the sound effects before."

Mr Price wasn't the only one to feel uneasy at the thought of Paddington taking part in his play and by the time the following evening came round everyone in the Brown household was in a high state of excitement as they got ready for their outing. Mr Price had been as good as his word and he'd not only given Paddington a number of tickets for the family, but he'd slipped in an extra one for Mr Gruber as well, and even Mr Curry had promised to put in an appearance.

Paddington went on ahead of the others as he had one or two last minute adjustments to make to his gramophone, but he was waiting at the door to greet them when they arrived just before the start of the performance. He was wearing a large rosette marked OFFICIAL in his hat and he looked most important as he led the way down the crowded aisle to some seats in the front row of the stalls, before disappearing through a small door at the side of the stage.

As the Browns settled down in their seats a roll of thunder shook the hall and Mrs Brown looked up anxiously. "That's very odd," she exclaimed. "Thunder at this time of the year. It was just starting to snow when we came in."

"I expect that was Paddington testing his sound effects," said Jonathan knowledgeably. "He said he had quite a few claps to do."

"Well, I wish he'd turn the volume down a bit," said Mrs Bird, turning her attention to the stage as the curtain began to rise. "That ceiling doesn't look too safe to me."

"I think someone must have forgotten to pay the electric light bill," whispered Mr Brown as he adjusted his glasses and peered at the scene.

Mr Price's play was called *The Mystery of Father Christmas and the Disappearing Plans* and according to the programme the action all took place one night in the hall of a deserted castle somewhere in Europe.

From where they were sitting the Browns not only found it difficult to see what was going on, but when their eyes did get accustomed to the gloom they found it even harder to understand what the play was about anyway.

Several times Father Christmas came through a secret panel in the wall holding a lighted candle in his hand, and each time he disappeared he was followed after a short interval by Mr Price playing the part of a mysterious butler. If Father Christmas was acting strangely Mr Price's actions were even more peculiar. Sometimes he came on waving the secret plans with a triumphant expression on his face, and at other times he looked quite sinister as he shook an empty fist at the audience to the accompaniment of a roll of thunder.

Behind the scenes Paddington was kept very busy. Apart from the thunder, there were the coconut shells to be banged together whenever anyone approached the castle, not to mention clanking drawbridge noises and creaking sounds each time a door was opened.

In fact there was so much to do it took him all his time to follow the script let alone watch the action on the stage and he was quite surprised when he looked up suddenly in the middle of one of his thunder records and found it was the interval.

"Very good work, Mr Brown," said Harold Price, as he came off the stage mopping his brow and stopped by Paddington's table. "I couldn't have done it better myself. I don't think you missed a single cue."

"Thank you very much," said Paddington, looking very pleased with himself as he returned Mr Price's thumb-up sign with a wave of his paw.

Quite a lot of people had come and gone

in the first half of Mr Price's play and altogether he wasn't sorry to sit down for a while and rest his paws. In any case the serfs had to put in several appearances during the second act and he was anxious to practise his lines while he had the chance.

It was some minutes after he had settled himself underneath the table with the script and a jar of marmalade that he noticed an unusual amount of noise going on at the back of the stage. It seemed to have something to do with Harold Price having mislaid his secret plans. Several times his voice rose above the others saying he couldn't go on without them because a lot of his most important lines were written on the back. Paddington scrambled out hurriedly in order to investigate the matter but by the time he stood up everything had gone quiet again and order seemed to have been restored as the curtain went up for the second act.

Paddington was looking forward to the second half of Mr Price's play and even though a lot of people were still creeping around behind the scenes with anxious expressions on their faces he soon forgot about it as Father Christmas made his entrance and approached Miss Flint's couch in the centre of the stage.

From the little that could be seen of him behind his beard, Father Christmas looked most unhappy as he addressed Miss Flint. "I had hoped to bring thee glad tidings," he cried, in ringing tones. "But alas, I am undone for *I have lost the secret plans!*"

"You've *what*?" exclaimed Miss Flint, jumping up from her couch in alarm. Miss Flint had spent the interval in her dressing-room and she was as surprised as anyone to learn that the plans really were missing. "What have you done with them?" she hissed.

"I don't know," said Father Christmas in a loud whisper. "I think I must have put them down somewhere.

"Er... nice weather we've been having lately," he continued in a loud voice as he played for time. "Hast thou read any good books lately?"

From his position at the side of the stage Paddington looked even more surprised than Miss Flint at the sudden turn of events. Mr Price had explained the play very carefully to him and he felt sure no mention had been made of any character called Tidings. Then there was the question of the cloak. Father Christmas appeared to be wearing his cloak in exactly the same way that he'd worn it all

through the play and yet he'd definitely said something about it having come undone. Paddington consulted his script several times in case he'd made a mistake, but the more he looked at it the more confused he became.

It was as he turned round to the desk in order to play one of his thunder records just to be on the safe side that he received yet another surprise, for there, lying in front of him, was a dog-eared pile of papers with the words SECRET PLANS – PROPERTY OF HAROLD PRICE written in large letters across the front.

Paddington looked at the papers and then back at the stage. A nasty silence seemed to have come over the audience, and even Father Christmas and Miss Flint appeared to have run out of conversation as they stared at each other in embarrassment.

Coming to a decision Paddington picked up the secret plans and hurried on to the stage with a determined expression on his face. After raising his hat several times to the audience he waved in the direction of the Browns and Mr Gruber and then turned towards the couch.

"Odds bodikins!" he cried, giving Father Christmas a hard stare. "I've come to do you up."

"You've come to do what?" repeated Father Christmas nervously, as he stood clutching the candle in one hand and the end of the couch in the other.

"I'm afraid I can't see anything about Glad Tidings in my script," continued Paddington. "But I've found your secret plans."

Paddington looked very pleased with

himself as a burst of applause came from the audience. "Scurvy knave!" he exclaimed, making the most of his big moment. "Gadzooks! You left them under my coconuts!"

"I left them *where*?" said Father Christmas in a daze, as Paddington held out the plans and he exchanged them for the candle.

"Under my coconuts," explained Paddington patiently. "I think you must have put them there in the interval."

"Fancy leaving your plans under a bear's coconuts," hissed Miss Flint. "A fine spy you are!"

While Miss Flint was talking a glassy look came over Father Christmas. So much had gone wrong already that evening it didn't seem possible anything else could happen, but there was definitely a very odd odour coming from somewhere.

"Can you smell something burning?" he asked anxiously.

Miss Flint paused. "Good heavens!" she cried, hurriedly taking the candle away from Paddington. "It's your beard – it's on fire!"

"It's all right, Mr Christmas, I'm coming," called Paddington as he climbed up on to the couch. "I think I must have held the wick too close by mistake."

A gasp of surprise went up from the audience as Paddington took hold of the beard and gave it a tug.

"Well I'm blowed," said a voice near the Browns, as the whiskers came away in Paddington's paws and revealed the perspiring face of Harold Price. "Fancy that! It was the butler all the time – disguised as Father Christmas!"

"What a clever idea," said a lady in the row behind. "Having him unmasked by a bear."

"A most unusual twist," agreed her companion.

"My play!" groaned Harold Price, collapsing into a chair and fanning himself with the secret plans as the curtain came down. "My masterpiece – ruined by a bear!"

"Nonsense!" exclaimed Miss Flint, coming to Paddington's rescue. "It wasn't Mr Brown's fault. If you hadn't lost the plans in the first place all this would never have happened. Anyway," she concluded, "the audience seem to like it – just listen to them."

Mr Price sat up. Now that Miss Flint mentioned it there did seem to be a lot of applause coming from the other side of the curtain. Several people were shouting

"Author" and someone even appeared to be making a speech.

"I feel," said the judge, as they joined him on the stage, "we must congratulate Harold Price on his pantomime. It was undoubtedly the funniest play of the week."

"The *funniest*," began Mr Price. "But it wasn't meant to be funny..."

The judge silenced him with a wave of his hand. "Not only was it the funniest, but it had the most unusual ending I've seen for many a day. That serf bear," he said, as he consulted a piece of paper in his hand, "his name doesn't seem to appear on the programme – but he played his part magnificently. Remarkable timing – the way he set light to your beard. One false move with his paw and the whole lot might have gone up in flames!

"I have no hesitation," he concluded, amid a long burst of applause from the audience, "in awarding the prize for the best play of the festival to Mr Harold Price."

Harold Price looked rather confused as the applause died away and someone called out "Speech".

"It's very kind of you all," he said, "and I'm most grateful. But I think I ought to mention that although I *wrote* the play, young Mr Brown here had quite a large paw in the way it ended.

"I shouldn't be standing here now if it wasn't for him," he added, as he turned to Paddington amid another outburst of clapping, "and I wouldn't like to think he'd gone unrecognized."

"How kind of Mr Price to give Paddington some of the credit," said Mrs Brown later that evening as they made their way home through the snow. "I wonder what he meant when he said Paddington had a paw in the ending?"

"Knowing Paddington's paws," said Mrs Bird, "I shudder to think."

Mr Gruber and the Browns looked back at Paddington in the hope of getting some kind of an explanation but his head was buried deep in his duffle coat and he was much too busy picking his way in and out of their footprints to hear what was being said.

Paddington liked snow, but while they'd been in the theatre rather too much had fallen for his liking and he was looking forward to warming his paws in front of the fire at number thirty-two Windsor Gardens.

Apart from that, the sight of a Christmas tree in someone's window had just reminded him of the date and he was anxious to get home as quickly as possible so that he could hang up his stocking.

There were still several more days to go before the holiday but after watching Mr Price's play that evening Paddington didn't want to take any chances, particularly over such an important matter as Father Christmas.